Gavin ran as fast as he could.

More rounds exploded around him. One hit its mark.

He yelled out in pain as the bullet seared into him.

Jamie had turned at the sound of his scream. She hurried to his side.

"We need to get out of sight before they reach the road." He pointed to the wooded area on the opposite side of the street. In his condition, it might as well be on the other side of the moon. He wasn't sure he could make it another foot.

Blood soaked Gavin's hand; his vision blurred. It was a struggle to keep from losing consciousness. He blinked hard and forced back the nausea.

Behind them, he could hear the men. They'd reached the road.

"Go ahead of me. Get to the house. Call for help." His words slurred. He couldn't hang on much longer.

Jamie ignored what he said. She put her arm around his waist and helped him along as best she could. He winced in pain, his strength slowly ebbing away. They had to reach the house. It was their only chance. If he passed out now, it was all over...

Mary Alford was inspired to become a writer after reading romantic suspense greats Victoria Holt and Phyllis A. Whitney. Soon, creating characters and throwing them into dangerous situations that tested their faith came naturally for Mary. In 2012 Mary entered the Speed Dating contest hosted by Love Inspired Suspense and later received "the call." Writing for Love Inspired Suspense has been a dream come true for Mary.

Books by Mary Alford

Love Inspired Suspense

Forgotten Past
Rocky Mountain Pursuit
Deadly Memories
Framed for Murder
Standoff at Midnight Mountain
Grave Peril

GRAVE PERIL

MARY ALFORD

HARLEQUIN® LOVE INSPIRED® SUSPENSE

Recycling programs
for this product may
not exist in your area.

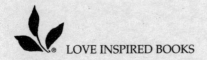

LOVE INSPIRED BOOKS

ISBN-13: 978-1-335-54407-0

Grave Peril

Copyright © 2018 by Mary Eason

Before the mountains were brought forth,
or ever thou hadst formed the earth and the world,
even from everlasting to everlasting, thou art God.
–Psalms 90:2

To anyone facing an insurmountable mountain
in their life. Know that God is with you
through each step of the way.

ONE

The rain that had followed Jamie Hendricks from Louisville came down harder as she reached the Appalachians. The mountains had a way of attracting dramatic weather. Today was no different. Dark gray storm clouds gathered atop Darlan Mountain, obscuring it from view and spreading spindly fingers of fog throughout the valley below.

Still, even in the growing darkness, the beauty of the mountains drew Jamie in, filling her with memories that were mostly good...until she thought about that horrible day.

In spite of everything she'd done to deny it, this was home.

Yet nothing about this trip was the heart-warming homecoming she'd longed for throughout the years.

I know who killed Charles Dalton...

Her uncle's chilling words were her constant

companion. She wouldn't be here now if it hadn't been for Uncle Paxton's call.

As soon as Jamie reached the sign for Darlan, Kentucky, at the city limits, she grabbed her cell phone. Once more, she tried to reach her uncle, like she had periodically since leaving Louisville. The lack of service surrounding the mountains did little to reassure her, and her uneasiness grew. Their last conversation dominated her thoughts, as did the fear she'd heard in his voice.

"Where are you, Uncle Paxton?" Frustrated, Jamie tossed the cell phone on the seat beside her.

As she drove down Main Street, the ugliness of the last year she'd spent here was everywhere around her. From Givens Grocery, where she'd first heard the whispers about her father's guilt from patrons of the store, to the cold stares she'd received from her classmates at Darlan High School at the end of the road. Her father had been convicted of killing Charles Dalton even before a jury of his peers passed judgment.

Losing her mother to cancer at five had been difficult, but watching her father being hauled away to prison for something he didn't do was devastating. An only child, Jamie and her father had become inseparable after her mother's death. Back then, she couldn't imagine her life without him in it.

It took everything inside Jamie not to turn the car around, ignore Uncle Paxton's concerns and head back to Louisville, where she'd tried to keep the past buried for so long.

Help me, Lord. I have to stay strong for my uncle.

Even though she was exhausted beyond belief, Jamie didn't make a single stop in town. Paxton needed her. She headed toward the county road that would lead up the mountainside to her family home, where he was waiting for her.

A part of her prayed Uncle Paxton had finally found the evidence needed to clear her father's name, while another part knew that, no matter what, the damage was written in stone. Her father's conviction had destroyed so many lives, Noah's included. And it had been the death knell for her future with Gavin.

As she headed up Darlan Mountain, the rain seemed determined to play its part in the story of her return, just as it had the day long ago when she'd left town, thinking it would be for good. Back then, it had been as if the skies themselves were weeping right along with Jamie.

Jamie switched the wipers to high as the downpour made it difficult to see. Fog descending from the mountaintop took away the rest of her visibility. It was as if she were driving blindfolded.

Growing up, there had been half a dozen families living up on the mountain. With the decline of coal mining in the county in recent times, that number had shrunk to only two.

Forced to slow the car's speed to a snail's crawl, Jamie passed the last house up the mountain before her family's home.

Don't look, her heart urged, yet Jamie couldn't help it. The Dalton home was dark save for a single light that appeared to be coming from the kitchen. Gavin was home, his reasons for returning to Darlan far worse than hers. He'd come back to bury his Grandmother Ava.

When Uncle Paxton first told Jamie about Ava's passing, she'd wanted to come home for the funeral, yet her last conversation with Gavin stood in the way. Ten years might have passed, but she hadn't been able to get those ugly parting words out of her head. She'd pleaded her father's innocence. Gavin hadn't believed her. Her seventeen-year-old heart had broken into a thousand pieces. In that same heart, Jamie had believed Gavin would not welcome her presence at Ava's funeral.

Edging around the side of the mountain, past the Dalton place, Jamie focused her entire attention on the limited view before her. Gavin was her past. She was here for her uncle.

Jamie barely cleared the curve when a set of headlights suddenly appeared in her rearview mirror, taking her by surprise and temporarily blinding her. Up until now, she hadn't seen a single soul since she'd reached Darlan.

The lights continued to grow bigger as she squinted. The driver appeared to be speeding up, in spite of the road conditions. What was he thinking, going so fast around such a dangerous corner?

Beyond the Dalton place, her family home was the only other house up on the mountain, and yet the vehicle continued to come on strong.

By now, the driver should have seen her and slowed down.

I know who killed Charles Dalton... Her last phone conversation with Uncle Paxton inserted itself into her thoughts, unwelcome.

In the driver's-side mirror, she was able to make out what appeared to be a monstrous SUV mirroring her every move. It wasn't Uncle Paxton's vehicle. He drove a truck.

Someone was following her.

Jamie reached for her cell phone again. But the service was nonexistent, and she wasn't sure who she would try to call. Paxton wasn't picking up, and the text message he'd sent soon after their final conversation warned her not to trust anyone from the sheriff's department.

Fear slithered into the pit of her stomach. She was on her own.

The vehicle quickly closed the space between them to within a few feet of her car, and the lights turned on bright. The driver was deliberately trying to intimidate her.

Jamie struggled to shut down the panic. If she wanted to survive, she'd have to figure a way out of this.

Uncle Paxton's worried declaration continued to niggle at her thoughts: *I'm in real trouble, Jamie. I know who killed Charles Dalton, and because of it they're coming after me!*

What had her uncle uncovered that had sent him into such a panic, and how was it connected to the person tailing her now?

Jamie moved as close to the edge of the road as safely possible, hoping she'd misunderstood the driver's intent and the vehicle would try to pass. It continued right on her bumper. She increased her speed. The SUV did the same. This was no misunderstanding.

If what Uncle Paxton said were true, his life could be in danger.

Red Plume Lane was just up ahead. If she could make it there, she could turn around and head back down the mountain. Hopefully get away before the driver tried something lethal. She didn't dare take Red Plume, as it dead-ended not too far past the intersection.

Jamie's hands tightened on the wheel. She spotted the road up on her left.

Please, Lord, help me...

It was now or never. With all her strength, Jamie whipped the steering wheel to her left and spun the car around, sliding on the wet road and almost losing control.

Somehow, she managed to keep the car from slipping off the road. Once it was straightened out, Jamie floored the gas and peered in her rearview mirror. She caught a glimpse of the vehicle turning around. The SUV was coming after her still. The other vehicle's powerful engine raced closer. There was only one option left. If she could reach Gavin's house, she knew—no matter what their past might be—he would help her.

Jamie watched in horror as the SUV lurched forward, its headlights growing huge before it rammed into the back of her car, throwing her forward.

She clutched the wheel tightly to keep the car from veering off the road. Her heart flew into her throat. The driver was deliberately trying to run her off the road.

Even with the gas pedal on the floor, her car was no match for the powerful SUV. Before her brain had time to process what to do next, the vehicle smashed into her again, this time harder than before. Her head slammed against the steering wheel. For a second, Jamie thought she would black out.

Her car swerved to the left and spun around. She fought to keep it on the road, but her efforts were futile as the car plunged nose first into the rain-filled ditch and the world around her blurred.

While Jamie held on to consciousness by a thread, she was vaguely aware of the SUV rolling to a stop beside her. The driver's door opened and she saw a man in khaki pants heading her way.

With her heart pouring adrenaline through her body, Jamie squeezed her eyes closed. If she pretended to be unconscious, maybe he wouldn't hurt her.

The man stopped next to her and opened the door. He leaned down. She could feel him studying her and was terrified he'd finish what he started and kill her right then and there.

"She's out cold. Check the back. Maybe she has some of it with her." He hit the trunk button and Jamie could hear it opening.

"There's nothing here," a second man said, then closed the trunk with a slam. "Doesn't look like he was ever with her. He's still out there somewhere. We'd better find him and the stuff before *he* arrives."

The man hovering over her still hadn't moved. Was he debating whether or not to kill her?

"Let her be. We don't need the hassle of covering up another murder. She didn't see anything, and we need to get out of here. There's a house down the mountain. They could have heard the noise."

After what felt like a lifetime, the man near her finally spoke. "Yeah, well, I hope you're right about that because I know her."

It took everything inside of Jamie not to react to those terrifying words. She thought she recognized the man's voice. He pretty much confirmed it.

While she kept as still as her heart would allow, the man finally moved away. With her eyes shut tight, she heard the SUV turn around and head up the mountain. They were going to her house!

We don't need the hassle of covering up another murder. They'd killed someone else. Her thoughts went to Gavin's father. Were these the men responsible for killing Charles? If so, then they were going after Uncle Paxton now.

Even with the noise of the engine fading in the distance, Jamie was terrified to move. It was the thought of what would happen when those two came back and decided to finish the job that finally forced her into action. She had to get out of there. Had to find Paxton.

Slowly, she opened her eyes. Her head ached. The world around her spun and her stomach threatened to heave. Squeezing her eyes closed, she waited until everything stopped spinning.

Smoke billowed from the wasted engine of her car. She was stranded out here on this secluded stretch of road, and she had no idea when her attackers might return.

As she struggled to free herself from the seatbelt, she felt blood oozing from a gash on her forehead. Her body ached from the jarring impact of the vehicle slamming into her.

Once she'd freed herself, Jamie grabbed her cell phone and scrambled out of the car. She fought to keep from passing out as she waded through the almost knee-deep water in the ditch up to the road.

The isolation of the area was far worse than she remembered. Her home was still a good mile up. With the vehicle out of commission, there was only one option left. She'd have to walk out.

The no-service indicator on her phone did little to ease her mind. Without knowing what those men would do to her when they came back down the mountain, she couldn't risk keeping to the road. She had to stay out of sight.

While she thought about her best route to stay hidden, another set of headlights rounded the bend in the road some distance down from her. Someone else was coming!

Jamie's heart slammed against her chest. She searched the surrounding darkness for somewhere to hide. The mountainside was covered in trees. She raced across the road and into the woods there.

The vehicle continued to advance at a much slower pace than the one following her. As she watched, a beat-up truck came to a stop behind her car. She couldn't see who was driving, and until she knew who it was, she wasn't about to come out of hiding.

It took a second for Jamie to regain her bearings. As a child, she'd played in these woods and knew them all by heart. As much as the idea of going to Gavin for help didn't appeal to her, there was no doubt that she needed it. Those men had been looking for Paxton and something else. He'd told her he'd be waiting for her at the house. If those men found him there, she couldn't imagine what they'd do to him.

Gavin Dalton pulled up as close behind the wrecked car as he could get, his headlights on bright. It sat nose first in a ditch, filled with water up to the floorboards. Smoke plumed from its engine. The driver's door stood open. It didn't look as if anyone was inside. Where had the driver gone?

Today of all days, this was the last thing he needed. He'd heard the noise that sounded like vehicles colliding up the mountain, and his conscience wouldn't let him not go to render aid.

Barring the day he'd buried his father, today had been the worst day of his life. He'd had to say goodbye to his beloved Grandmother Ava. Even after seeing her in the casket, he still couldn't believe his rock was gone. She'd practically raised him. He'd never really known his mother, since she'd died when he was still a baby, right up here on this same mountain. Her car had run off the road one winter's day. It had been just Gavin, his dad and Ava for as long as he could remember.

When he got the call that Ava had passed, it had floored him. Ava had suffered a massive heart attack while sitting out back on her favorite bench, no doubt watching the sunset over Darlan Mountain, as she had for going on seventy years.

Gavin had been doing the same thing minutes earlier when he'd heard the crash.

As a CIA agent, he'd seen a lot of bad things. His instincts just naturally veered toward trouble. Turned out, this time he was right.

While he continued to stare at the wreckage before him, he noticed something that didn't jibe with the car ending up in the ditch of its own accord. The back bumper was crumpled in several spots. It appeared someone had deliberately forced it off the road. He scanned the area. His concern for the missing driver doubled.

Always lend a hand, Gavin. Mountain folk look out for one another. He could almost hear his grandmother reminding him of this. Ava had lived that creed throughout her life. *She* never once failed to lend a hand when someone was in need.

Even though he'd been gone for ten years, he understood why Ava had loved this place so much. It was in her blood. His, too. This was one of the reasons it was so hard to think about selling her home. Still, now that she was gone, he couldn't imagine living there, and his job as a member of the CIA specialized antiterrorist unit known as the Scorpions took him out of the country for months at a time.

Excuses…all of them. The real reason he didn't want to hold on to the house was that he saw his father everywhere around the place. The brutal way Charles Dalton's life had been taken from him would forever mar Gavin's memories of life on the mountain. Shot to death by his best friend and business partner.

And so he'd come to a difficult decision. He planned to get in touch with the local real estate agent the next day. Put the house on the market and see what happened.

Now, as he took in the extent of damage to the car, he realized there was a good chance that whoever was driving the vehicle had been injured.

With that disturbing thought still ringing in his head, Gavin grabbed his flashlight and got out, clicking the light on. Tucking his service weapon behind his back, he waded into the water and slowly eased to the open door.

As he approached, the empty driver's seat confirmed that no one was inside. He shone the flashlight into the back seat. There was a suitcase and what looked like a laptop bag. In the passenger's seat, a purse. The sight increased his unease. Why would the driver leave her identification behind?

Gavin pulled out the wallet tucked inside the purse. The name on the driver's license froze him in place and sent his heart back in time. Jamie Hendricks. The car in question belonged to his high school sweetheart. The woman he'd once loved with all his heart.

He glanced frantically around. Where was she?

Jamie wouldn't have simply walked off for help without taking her purse or locking the car up with her belongings inside. He flashed the light around, yet there was no sign she might have been thrown from the car.

What if Jamie been taken against her will by the driver of the second vehicle? His gut clenched at the thought.

He remembered his grandmother telling him about how much the crime rate had increased over the past ten years in Darlan due to the flood of drugs rolling through the community.

Gavin whispered a prayer for a safe outcome, then went into action.

"Jamie!" he yelled as loud as he could, hoping she could hear him if she was still close by. His voice echoed down into the valley below. "Jamie, it's Gavin Dalton!"

Across the road, something rustled in the bushes. It could be a wild animal. Hogs were everywhere around these hollers. He homed the flashlight in on the direction of the noise and saw movement.

With his heart wrenching like crazy, he yelled, "Put your hands in the air and show yourself before I shoot! Now!"

He kept the flashlight focused on the parting bushes as someone—a woman—emerged. She squinted as the light hit her eyes. One hand went up to shield them.

It had been ten years since he'd last seen her,

but he'd thought about her—and what might have been—just about every day of his life.

Seeing her now felt almost surreal. He couldn't believe Jamie was back in Darlan and that someone had run her into the ditch.

She ran across the road and into his arms. He could feel her shivering in reaction to what had just taken place, as well as to the chill of the night air.

Time melted away as he held her tighter. She still felt the same in his arms as she had all those years ago. They'd been so close once. He'd planned to ask her to marry him the summer before they were both scheduled to leave for university.

And then *that* day happened. His world had changed forever when her father killed his. Their life together and the future he'd once envisioned for them had splintered into a million pieces. A chasm stood between them that was impossible to breach. For the first time in their lives, they'd stood on opposite sides of something.

Gavin pulled himself together and moved a little away so that he could get a good look at her. Even terrified, she was still the prettiest girl he'd ever known. Her normally sparkling green eyes reflected the horror of what she'd gone through tonight.

She had a bloody gash on her forehead. Clumps of her golden-brown hair were matted into it.

Jamie drew in a breath and took a step back, as if realizing what she'd done. Gavin let her go. The lethal past was firmly in place between them once again.

"I was scared they were coming back again. Gavin, someone ran me off the road." Her voice shook. He didn't doubt for a second how terrifying the experience had been.

"You're hurt." His immediate attention went to her injury. He examined the gash gently with his fingertips and couldn't keep the anger from his tone. Someone had tried to harm her, and he had no idea why.

She drew in a shaky breath and pulled away from his touch. "No, I'm fine. It just scared me."

"Jamie, you're not. That looks like it needs stiches." He indicated the wound, but she shook her head, trying to play the injury down.

"I'll be fine. It looks worse than it is."

While he doubted it, he knew it was pointless to argue. Jamie could be stubborn when she wanted to.

"I heard the crash from my place. What happened?"

She was shaking so much that it appeared to be a struggle to get words to come out. "I'm not sure. I was driving home when an SUV came out of nowhere. I thought it was just some kids playing around until they forced me off the road."

He didn't want to believe she'd been deliberately targeted in such a frightening way. "Are you sure it was on purpose? The road is wet. It's hard to see with the rain and the fog."

She waved his theory away. "I'm positive. Gavin, they were inches from my bumper the whole time. When I tried to turn around and get to your place, they rammed my car twice. The last time I lost control, and that's when I was run off the road by two men."

He frowned at her answer. It was not the one he'd wanted to hear. "Did you get a good look at the vehicle?"

She shook her head. "Not really. It happened so fast. I know it was an SUV and that it was big. And I think it was black or maybe dark brown."

It wasn't much to go on. "After you crashed in the ditch, did the SUV keep going?" He hadn't heard the vehicle drive past his house.

She hesitated, sending a bunch of alarm signals up for him. "Yes. They're heading up to my house."

He stared at her, trying to understand the meaning. "Why would they be heading to your house...?" Then it finally clicked. "Where's Paxton?"

"He's supposed to meet me there. Gavin, we have to help him. I'm afraid they'll hurt him."

His thoughts reeled. Why had someone tried

to hurt her or Paxton? "What's Paxton gotten himself involved in this time?" Gavin couldn't keep the hard edge from his tone.

"I wish I knew." She didn't look at him, leaving him with the impression she wasn't telling the whole story. Jamie didn't trust him. That hurt to consider.

His mouth tightened in revulsion as he thought about how bad the outcome of the wreck could have been.

"What aren't you telling me, Jamie? There's no way what happened to you here doesn't involve one of Paxton's harebrained theories in some way."

She finally faced him, her defiance clear. "I told you I don't know anything, so will you help me or not?"

Before he could answer, the noise of another vehicle coming up the mountain interrupted their conversation.

Jamie turned frightened eyes to him. "What if it's connected to the other vehicle? We have to get out of here now."

She was right. Standing on the side of the road like this, they were exposed, sitting targets. Together, they hurried back to his truck. Before they had the chance to get inside, red and blue lights flashed behind them.

Relief swept through Gavin. "It's okay. It's the sheriff."

Yet, instead of relaxing, Jamie appeared more panicked. She shook her head. "No, Gavin, we have to get out of here now. Uncle Paxton warned me not to trust anyone at the sheriff's office."

Hearing her uncle's claims, Gavin's distrust grew. Paxton had been on a mission to prove his brother hadn't killed Charles ever since the man had been convicted of the crime. When Noah died of miner's lung two years into his life sentence, Paxton's efforts had gone into overdrive. He'd even enlisted his good friend, Gavin's grandmother, Ava Dalton, in the hunt for evidence.

Before Gavin had time to ask why Paxton didn't trust the sheriff's office, the patrol vehicle chirped its siren once then pulled alongside the truck.

Gavin grabbed her hand and squeezed it. "Let me handle this."

The passenger window came down. A shockwave rolled through Gavin upon identifying the man sitting inside the white police SUV. Andy Lawson was the last person Gavin would have expected to be elected sheriff of Darlan County, in spite of the fact that his father had once held the position.

He and Andy had gone through their entire

school years together. Andy was a borderline juvenile delinquent whose father had had to bail him out of trouble throughout most of his high school years. Gavin couldn't imagine how this man had become sheriff, except on his father's merits.

Andy seemed about as shocked to see Gavin. "Gavin Dalton? I heard you were back in town. Sorry to hear about your grandmother. She was a great gal."

"Thanks, man." Gavin somehow got the words out. He knew good and well Andy and his grandmother had never gotten along. Ava had been very vocal about Andy's lack of discipline and had spoken to his father about it on numerous occasions.

At one time, the Lawsons lived on the mountain before moving to town. Their property backed onto to Ava's. When Gavin was younger, Ava had run cattle on that part of the place. Through the years, several head had gone missing. Ava was convinced Andy had had something to do with it. Gavin and his dad were inclined to agree, but without hard proof tying Andy to the missing cattle, there had been no way to prove it.

Andy looked past Gavin and spotted Jamie. "I didn't see you there, Jamie. I had no idea you were back in town, too. Is this your car? Looks like you had a doozy of a wreck. Are you hurt?"

Gavin could feel Jamie's unease growing. She managed to shake her head. "No, I'm fine."

"What happened here?" Andy asked, still without even looking at the car. Immediately, his lack of interest in the car's obvious damage garnered Gavin's concern. As far as he could tell, the man hadn't given it more than a cursory glance. As a sheriff, it was an odd way to investigate an accident. Unless he already knew about what happened and was checking to see if Jamie was still alive?

"It was my fault, I'm afraid." Gavin jumped in with a made-up explanation to get Andy's attention off Jamie. "I accidently hit Jamie. I was taking a ride up the mountain when I came to the bend. I guess I was going a little too fast for the road conditions, and I tagged her."

"Have you talked to Paxton lately?" Andy's immediate change of subject surprised them both.

Jamie edged closer to Gavin. "No...why?"

"No reason," Andy answered a little too quickly. "I just had a few more questions for him since he was the one who found Ava after she died." He frowned. "Why are you back in Darlan, anyway? Did you come for the funeral?"

Jamie quickly grasped at the excuse he'd provided. "Yes, that's right."

Gavin wasn't surprised that Andy hadn't been at his grandmother's funeral, considering their past relationship, but neither Jamie nor Paxton had attended, either. Not that he could blame Jamie after the way things ended between them. Still, Paxton had been a good friend of Ava's. Unless he hadn't been able to attend because he'd gotten himself into trouble.

Andy accepted her answer without questioning it. "Well, if you see him, tell him I'd like to have a word. You need me to call a tow truck to get you out of the ditch?"

Something was definitely off with Andy's way of handling the whole situation, and Gavin was anxious to get rid of him. "No, that's okay. I'll give Marty a call and have him pull it out for Jamie."

After another suspicious look, Andy nodded. "Alright, then. If you two don't need me, I'm heading home. My shift just ended a little while ago. I was at the end of the road by the intersection when I heard the ruckus up here and decided to come check it out. Glad I did. You need a ride to your house, Jamie? I'd be happy to give you a lift. That way I can check in with Paxton. Get the answers I need and then be on my way."

"You can't," Jamie said in a rush, then amended

her answer when Andy appeared more suspicious. "What I mean is, he's not home. He went to Jamesville for a few days to gather supplies for the mine."

"You don't say… That was kind of sudden, wasn't it?" Andy scowled at her answer. He'd come just short of calling her a liar.

Gavin stepped in. "I can give Jamie a ride. You're on your way home, and since Paxton's not there, anyway, it would be a wasted trip." He'd seen that Andy knew Jamie wasn't telling him the truth. Would he push to go to her house? If so, Gavin wasn't about to let Jamie head up there alone with Andy.

"Suit yourself," Andy mumbled, finally ending the silent standoff. "Have Paxton call me when you talk to him, you hear?"

Jamie nodded.

Andy put the vehicle in gear and gave them a two-finger salute before making a U-turn in the middle of the road to head back down the mountain.

Once he was gone, Jamie let out a huge sigh. "I don't trust him for a minute. He was definitely fishing for something." She looked as pale as a sheet.

Gavin had a dozen different questions running though his mind. "Why does Andy need to talk to Paxton so urgently? I spoke to the coroner. Ava had a heart attack, and that caused her death. Even though Paxton found her, what questions could he possibly still have?" He watched Jamie closely. "Did Paxton tell you anything else about my grandmother's death?"

She appeared frazzled by the events of the evening. "No, only that Ava had died and he was the one who found her."

None of it added up in Gavin's mind. Why was the sheriff so concerned with finding Paxton?

His gaze narrowed. As far as he knew, Jamie hadn't been home once since she'd left, with the exception of attending her father's funeral.

"What else did Paxton say to get you to come back here? It had to be big." There was no disguising the bitterness in his tone. He couldn't help it. Her sudden exit from his life had been eating at him for years.

The way things had ended between them after the trial, well, it had been devastating for him as well as her. Gavin knew he was mostly to blame for it. He'd been grieving for his father while Jamie kept insisting that Noah was innocent. He hadn't been able to handle it any longer and lost his temper. Told her he didn't believe her. That he'd never believe her. It had been the end of them. He'd always regretted saying that to her. Even though it was the truth, it added yet another wedge between them that made it impossible to overcome. He'd hoped that once things settled, he and Jamie could work things out. That hadn't happened.

The tears in her eyes as she'd looked at him still haunted him. That had been the last time he saw her, standing in front of her family home, begging him to believe her.

Jamie left town without so much as a word, and his future happiness crumbled around him.

He'd moved away shortly afterward, to attend university, and then later joined the CIA. They'd both left Darlan behind, and now the only family member tying him here was gone.

Like Jamie's Uncle Paxton, his grandmother had never believed Noah Hendricks murdered her son. She'd gone along with every single one of Paxton's crazy ideas to clear Noah's name, much to Gavin's dismay. It was about the only thing he and his grandmother had ever argued about. In Gavin's mind, there had been no other explanation. Noah had shot his father when he found out Charles was thinking of selling the mine he owned to a large corporation.

Jamie didn't look at him when she answered. "He said he had finally found proof that would exonerate my father of killing Charles. I know what you're thinking, but this time there was something in his voice." She intercepted his disbelieving look. "I can feel it, Gavin. This time I believe he really knows who killed your father."

Gavin ran his hand across the back of his neck. "Jamie, we both know who killed my dad. Just because Paxton and you can't accept it doesn't mean it isn't true."

She squared her shoulders and took him on, arguing her case. "Your grandmother didn't believe Noah was capable of killing Charles. Your own grandmother."

He'd heard enough. "Jamie, a jury of Noah's peers convicted him of the crime, remember?" When tears filled her eyes, he regretted his outburst. "Look, I'm sorry it happened. I loved your dad. He was like family…until, well, you know. And I'm sorry he had to pass away in prison like that. I can't imagine how that was for him and for you. But it's time both Paxton and you let go of this vendetta and got on with your lives. Before what Noah did that day poisons what's left of them."

TWO

No matter what the jury had said, Jamie would never believe the kind and gentle man she remembered her father being would ever be capable of harming his good friend Charles.

She choked back old memories from childhood. Her father used to read her stories from the Bible each night before she went to sleep. Even when her mother was still alive, the bedtime Bible reading was *their* time together. Her father was a Godly man. Noah never once missed a church service, and was a deacon for most of his adult life. Noah Hendricks went out of his way to help anyone in need.

So it didn't matter what the jury declared or what Gavin chose to believe; Noah and Charles had been much closer than friends. They'd been like brothers. And Noah would never hurt his brother.

Yet it was pointless to have this ugly conversation with Gavin again. They'd gone over it a dozen times in the past. She'd pled her father's cause with all her heart, and Gavin hadn't believed her.

The anger simmering in his eyes told her nothing had changed. But Gavin had. He'd left here a sweet young boy who'd stolen her heart. The man standing before her now had a hard edge about him.

He was still as handsome as ever, with straight blond hair that touched the collar of his shirt. A good six inches taller than she was, Gavin had been a star athlete in high school. He still looked as if he could run a football.

Jamie forced her straying thoughts back to the moment. "Uncle Paxton could be in real trouble by now."

Gavin blew out a frustrated-sounding sigh. "Come on. Let's get you inside the truck where it's warm." He reached for her arm, but she shook him off. "Jamie, I'm not letting you walk into what could prove to be a dangerous situation. I'll take you to my house where you can warm up, and then I'll go and check on Paxton." He headed for the driver's side of the truck, but she didn't budge. Gavin turned back. "Jamie…"

There was no way she was going anywhere but to look for Paxton. "I'm going home. Paxton needs me. If you won't take me there, then I'll walk."

He stared at her as if she'd lost her mind. "Jamie, it's a good mile up the mountain still."

She lifted her chin. "Will you take me home, or do I walk?" Staring up at the man she'd once thought she would spend the rest of her life with, she realized how young and naive she'd been back then. So foolish. Or maybe it was just a matter of their circumstances simply being too much for them to overcome.

Gavin's blond hair was soaked through, as was the Stetson that looked like the same one he'd owned ten years ago. There were lines that hadn't been there on the younger Gavin's face, but the velvet-brown eyes were still the same, and when he looked at her, she could almost picture the old Gavin. Her Gavin. The carefree one who always caused her heart to do a little somersault.

"Okay, I'll take you," he bit out, clearly not happy with the turn of events. "I'll go get your things from the car and then I'll take you home." He'd always called her stubborn when she was standing up for something she believed in. Especially when it was something they disagreed on.

It was that same stubbornness that had seen her through to becoming a criminal defense attorney and pursuing her passion of working to help those wrongfully convicted…like Noah.

Her father was right there with her through each new case she took on.

Gavin waited until she had gotten into the truck before slamming the door a little harder than necessary.

She watched him tramp down the damp road then wade into the ditch to get her things. He'd changed a lot since she'd been gone. Grown up. Matured.

He grabbed her purse from the front seat and then took out her bag and laptop and headed back to the truck.

Opening the rear door, he placed her things inside, took off his hat, then got behind the wheel.

"I'll call Marty Roberts when we get service. He can tow your car out of the ditch and get it home for you tomorrow. Maybe he can recommend a good repair shop in town."

"Thanks," she said and managed a smile. She could almost hear the remorse in his voice. Did he regret his earlier outburst?

She wondered if Gavin had kept in touch with Marty or any of his high school friends after he left town. Somehow, she doubted it. Like her, Gavin had cut ties, keeping his contact limited to only Ava.

Their gazes locked. After a moment he smiled, and her breath stuck in her throat. She'd forgotten how much she loved that smile.

"What's on your mind?" he asked when she continued to stare at him, mesmerized. Her heart drummed like crazy. Memories, both good and bad, gathered in her mind. The way things had ended with Gavin stunted her ability to form any lasting relationships. Jamie had thrown herself into her work, each new case taking a little bit more of her soul. The injustice she'd seen was heartbreaking.

One case, in particular, still haunted her. It was the first one she'd ever worked, an elderly man accused of killing his wife. The man had already served thirty years in prison when she found him. Jamie and her team worked hard to get him exonerated and gain his freedom. He'd died a few days later.

Jamie looked away and cleared her throat. "Nothing. I was just thinking about Ava. I'm sorry, Gavin. She was a sweet woman, and I loved her a bunch. She'll be missed."

Through the years, Jamie had kept in touch with Ava, who had been like a grandmother to her, as well. The only subject that she refused to discuss with the elderly woman was her grandson. It had taken a couple of phone calls before Ava finally relented on that topic. Still, she always insisted that Gavin loved Jamie, that she just needed to give him time to recover from the loss of his father.

But there had been one thing that Ava didn't know. Jamie hadn't had the courage to tell her about her last conversation with Gavin.

"Thanks," Gavin managed by way of an answer and returned his focus to the road ahead.

Jamie recalled how Ava had practically raised him, with Charles and Noah spending so much time at the coal mine trying to make it a success. She couldn't even imagine how hard Ava's death had been for him.

Because of the details of her grandson's life that Ava had dropped into their numerous conversations, Jamie knew Gavin had joined the CIA. He was fighting terror. Ava was so proud of her grandson.

"How long are you staying in Darlan?" she asked when he didn't make an effort to say anything more.

He glanced her way again, some of the hardness leaving his face. "Not long. I'm just settling Ava's affairs. I'll be putting her house up for sale, and then I'm heading back to Colorado." His voice was rough with emotion. She could see how hard this decision had been for him.

It tore at Jamie's heart to think of someone else living in Ava's home, but mostly because if Gavin was selling the place, it meant he was leaving town for good this time. That hurt like crazy. Part of her had always hoped there would be a second chance for them in the future, even though her life was in Louisville and his was in Colorado. She wanted to cry for the younger Jamie, whose heart had been torn beyond repair.

Somehow, she'd let go of the pain. She had no right to blame him for moving on. After all, she'd done the same. Jamie hadn't been back to Darlan since her father's funeral. The only time she saw Paxton was when he came to visit her in Louisville.

Besides, Gavin was her past. Her future was the law. She'd devoted herself to righting the wrongs of the justice system because she couldn't bear for another innocent person to die in prison like her father had.

When she couldn't think of a single thing to say to fill the silence, she turned her focus to her last conversation with her uncle. There had been something in Uncle Paxton's voice. She'd never heard him sound so afraid before.

He'd told her he knew who killed Charles, and yet when she'd questioned him about it, he'd refused to talk over the phone. Instead, he'd begged her to come home. Said he needed her. Had he been afraid of someone listening in on his conversations? Someone from the sheriff's office, maybe?

Gavin rounded the final bend and her house appeared off to the right of the dead end. Not a single light was on in the place. Uncle Paxton had promised to be here, yet his truck was nowhere in sight. Neither was the SUV that had run her into the ditch. Where had those men gone? There was no other way down the mountain except the road they'd come up or cross-country.

The rainy night kept the moon and the stars from providing light. The isolation of the area sent a chill speeding down her spine.

Gavin stopped the truck in front of the house and stared up at its darkness.

"I thought you said Paxton was meeting you here. Where's his truck? And where is the vehicle that ran you off the road? I don't like it, Jamie. Something's wrong." Gavin scanned the surrounding countryside. "The men in the SUV must have gone cross-country."

Was Paxton with them, or had he managed to escape?

Gavin put the truck in Reverse.

"What are you doing? We can't leave," she said in a panic when he backed out of the drive. "We have to find him."

He pointed to the opposite side of the road. "We need to get this truck out of sight. After what happened to you and our run-in with Andy Lawson, I don't like being out in the open like this."

Gavin slowly pulled the truck into the woods so it was out of sight and yet they still faced the house.

Once he'd parked, he stared up at the house with the same worry written on his face that she knew was on hers.

"Give me a second to check things out, then I'll come get you when I know it's clear." When she didn't respond, he looked over at her. "Jamie?"

Jamie couldn't answer because something alarming had caught her attention. A light in the woods close by. "What is that?" She pointed to it. Was it Paxton roaming the woods, hurt, or was it something far more deadly? Maybe it was the men who'd run her off the road, searching for Paxton.

She could see the uneasy set of Gavin's jaw. "Stay here while I go check it out," he said in a clipped tone. "Make sure you lock the door, and don't open it for anything or anybody. I'll be right back." Gavin got out of the truck. It was then that she noticed the gun he'd tucked inside the waist of his jeans.

He started to shut the door and suddenly the seriousness of the situation hit home and Jamie was afraid for him. She grabbed his arm. He stopped. Looked into her eyes. Her chest grew tight. She couldn't say what she really wanted to. Couldn't bring the past up again.

"Be careful." She breathed a little unsteadily. Their eyes held for a moment longer. She'd have given anything to know what he was thinking right then.

He slowly nodded and closed the door, waiting for her to lock it before he hurried away.

Jamie stared up at the house that had been her home for so long. Where was Uncle Paxton? And why was the sheriff so determined to speak with him?

Her thoughts churned with all the unanswered questions. The man in the SUV knew her. She'd recognized his voice. But trying to make sense out of something that was beyond her understanding without talking to Paxton was useless.

The darkness of the house was alarming. A disturbing thought came to her. What if Uncle Paxton was hurt inside? Maybe he'd hidden his truck somewhere and hiked in, worried that someone might be watching the place. If the men had gone inside and found him… She didn't want to think about what might have happened.

Ignoring Gavin's warning to stay in the truck, Jamie opened the door and got out.

She hadn't set foot inside her childhood home since her father's funeral. The dark windows and lack of light coming from inside sent chills down her spine and did little to ease her fears.

Jamie kept replaying her last conversation

with her uncle. Paxton had been frantic. After ten years of searching for evidence to clear Noah of murder, Paxton believed he'd located it. Why now, after so long?

She'd lost track of the numerous theories her uncle had come up with through the years. But this time felt different. What happened on the road back there seemed to back up the feeling.

Jamie continued to stare up at her old home as the rain soaked through her jacket and into her bones. Up here in the Appalachian Mountains, night came quickly and thoroughly. There was no light to keep the darkness at bay, making it hard to see your hand in front of you.

Her foot had just cleared the first step when Jamie noticed something she hadn't before. The front door stood ajar. Unease scurried down her spine. She could still hear the fear in her uncle's voice when he'd called to beg her to come home.

"Uncle Paxton, are you in there?" Jamie called out. The only answer was the familiar noises of the mountains. Locusts chirped. Somewhere close by an owl hooted. She could no longer hear Gavin moving through the woods. How long had he been gone? Was he in trouble?

The usually breathtaking night sky was obscured by clouds. The dampness of the mountains sent chill bumps up her arms.

She grabbed her cell phone. This time, the

phone picked up enough service for her to make the call. She dialed her uncle's number. Inside the house, Paxton's phone rang and then went to voicemail. Paxton never went anywhere without his phone.

Jamie's feet felt glued in place. Something was wrong.

She needed God's strength to push her legs into motion. Her uncle could be hurt.

With her prayer for courage chilling the night air, her heart thundered as each creaky step took her up to the gaping door.

Drawing in a deep breath, Jamie pushed the door the rest of the way open. She swallowed back fear and stepped inside. The house was pitch black, but what she could make out scared the daylights out of her. The room was in complete disarray. Furniture was turned over. All the drawers on her father's old antique desk stood open. Some had been pulled out completely.

Someone had ransacked the house. They'd been looking for something.

Jamie tried the light switch. Nothing happened. The power was off. Was it just a coincidence—or something more?

"Uncle Paxton, where are you?" she yelled one more time, knowing it was pointless. Her uncle wasn't here. Whether by his own will or someone else's, he was gone.

She spotted his phone lying on the floor and picked it up. The last call he'd made was to her, hours earlier.

Apprehension filled the pit of her stomach, and she looked nervously around the place. She'd been foolish to come here alone, going against Gavin's warning. Now she was on her own, and someone had obviously been here recently.

Jamie headed for the door, the hair on her arms standing at attention, the need to run overwhelming. She'd barely gotten halfway across the living room when someone grabbed her from behind, restraining her in a vice grip. Jamie screamed and clawed at the man's arm, but it was pointless. She was no match for his strength. He clamped a hand over her mouth to silence her.

Behind her, what sounded like a scuffle took place, then another man grabbed Paxton's phone, which she still clutched in her hand. "I've got *his* phone. Let's get him out of here now," she heard the man say. It was the same voice from earlier!

The man restraining her shoved her away hard. She stumbled forward. Before she could regain her footing, something smashed against her temple.

Jamie dropped to the floor, disoriented. The last thought she had before she lost consciousness was that she was here alone, and something bad had happened to her uncle.

* * *

In the distance, Gavin picked up the noise of what sounded like a four-wheeler's engine firing. The light he'd been following for a quarter of a mile disappeared, returning the mountain to its previous darkness.

Did it belong to someone out hunting, or was it connected to what had happened to Jamie earlier? He didn't believe in coincidences this big. Whoever was out here was up to no good.

Gavin headed for the last place he'd seen the light. The house behind him was still dark. Jamie had expected Paxton to be waiting for her there. Part of Gavin prayed that this would turn out to be just another one of Paxton's ridiculous theories.

Out of the corner of his eye, he caught movement. Gavin whirled in that direction, his flashlight in one hand, his weapon in the other. "Don't move or I'll shoot!"

A man he didn't recognize froze where he stood. Gavin kept the light aimed in his eyes as he moved closer. The man squinted against the brightness, but did as asked and stood motionless.

"What are you doing up here?" Gavin asked without lowering his weapon.

The man hesitated, no doubt trying to come up with a believable answer.

"Nothing. I was just doing some squirrel hunting. This type of weather is perfect for it. Can you lower the light and the weapon, buddy? I'd hate to get shot for no reason."

Gavin didn't buy his story for a second, and he sure wasn't prepared to lower his gun until he knew what the man was up to.

"Oh, yeah? Well, you're on private property. Did you get permission from the owner to be out here?" Gavin knew the answer already.

The man appeared sheepish. "No, sir, I didn't. But I figured the owner wouldn't mind if I rustled up a little food for the table."

Gavin noticed that the man didn't have a shotgun with him, but he caught sight of a bulge beneath his jacket. "What do you know about what happened down the road tonight?"

The man grew visibly ill at ease at the mention of the wreck. He edged closer to Gavin.

"That's far enough," Gavin warned.

The man stopped dead in his tracks. "I don't know what you're talking about. Look, I'm sorry to be hunting on your property and all. It won't happen again." He turned to leave through the woods behind him, but Gavin put a stop to it.

"Not so fast." In the distance, a single gunshot reverberated through the night. The man stopped dead. Gavin flashed his light in the direction of the shot. Nothing moved.

"Who else is out here with you?" Gavin demanded. When the man made no move to answer, Gavin edged closer with his gun aimed at the man's chest. "You need to come with me. Now."

The man took a step closer. "Alright, don't shoot. I'll come with you. But for the record, whoever fired that shot isn't connected to me."

Gavin pointed the gun in front of him. "Get moving."

The man made to move past Gavin, then grabbed a log from the ground and whirled around, slamming it hard against Gavin's side. Pain raced from the contact point down the side of his body. As he was stunned by the attack, the man had the advantage and kicked Gavin on his injured side. Gavin dropped to the ground, his breath leaving his body in a whoosh.

Through the pain, Gavin could just see the man running away as fast as he could. Before he reached the woods, two other people emerged from the direction of the shot, and the three disappeared from sight.

Gavin dragged himself to his knees. Holding his injured side, he drew in air and waited for the world to settle before he slowly staggered to his feet.

There was no doubt in his mind that the man

had been lying. He'd been up to no good, and so had his partners.

With his legs threatening to give out underneath him, Gavin took off in the direction the men had gone. He'd traveled a short distance when he realized that he was heading back to the road he and Jamie had just come up, only a little way from her house.

Once he reached the edge of the woods, he spotted the road and started down it. Another vehicle was parked behind tree coverage and out of sight from the road. A dark SUV, like the one Jamie described earlier.

Before Gavin could reach the vehicle, the driver fired the engine, splitting the quiet of the night. They were getting away. He ran toward the vehicle. The driver apparently spotted him and shoved the SUV into Drive and the car went screaming down the mountainside.

Gavin stopped in the middle of the road and stared after it. Who were these men, and why were they coming after Paxton?

He headed back in the direction he'd come. *He said he had finally found proof that would exonerate my father...*

What had Paxton uncovered that would make him believe he could clear Noah's name after all these years?

A chilling thought occurred to him. What had

the man who'd fired the shot been shooting at? Had they been inside Paxton's house? Fear raced through his body. He'd left Jamie sitting outside alone.

Gavin started running as fast as he could through the woods toward Paxton's house, ignoring the pain in his side. Whoever had forced Jamie off the road would have knowledge of her relationship with Paxton. They'd known where she was going tonight. Had they been waiting for her at the house to finish the job?

When he reached the clearing beside the house he noticed there were still no lights on inside. He rounded the corner and spotted the truck. Nothing moved so he hurried over. Jamie was nowhere in sight. There was little doubt in his mind that she'd gone looking for her uncle inside the house.

Gavin rushed up the steps. The door stood open. Inside, nothing but darkness greeted him. As his eyes adjusted, something moved close to the sofa. He drew his weapon, then he heard a moan and realized it was Jamie lying on the floor. She was hurt.

He dropped down to his knees beside her, his heart in his throat. "Jamie, are you okay?"

Please, God...

Slowly, she opened her eyes and stared up at

him with terror on her face. She tried to sit up, but he stopped her.

"Don't try to move. We don't know how serious that wound is. Coupled with what happened earlier, you could be hurt. I'm calling for help." He reached for his cell phone to dial 911, but she stopped him.

"No… Gavin, you can't." She struggled to a sitting position. Her fingers probed a spot on the left side of her head. "Gavin, they have Uncle Paxton."

He stared at her, trying to comprehend what she meant. "What do you mean, they have Paxton?"

"Someone came up behind me and grabbed me. They took Uncle Paxton's phone, and I think they took him hostage, as well. Before I knew what was happening, they hit me with something." She shivered when she spotted the fireplace poker lying nearby. "They came here looking for Paxton. I'm positive they found him."

There was no doubt in his mind that whoever had come after Paxton was connected to the men he'd run into. The man with the light had probably been stationed out back as a lookout.

He shared his misgivings. "He was probably part of the group I came across in the woods out back. I'm sure they're the same ones who ran you off the road earlier. They were driving a large SUV…"

He stopped when he remembered the gunshot. *They came here looking for Paxton. I'm positive they found him.*

His gaze held hers. "Jamie, I heard them shooting at something."

Her hand flew to cover her mouth. "Oh, please no. Gavin, Uncle Paxton could be hurt. We have to go after them."

He blew out an exasperated sigh. "We don't know where they were headed. We need help. These guys are obviously dangerous."

She shook her head before he even finished the thought. "No. For all we know, they're acting on Andy Lawson's orders. I told you Paxton warned me that, no matter what happened, I shouldn't reach out to the sheriff. There had to be a reason for the warning. After everything that happened here tonight, I believe him."

Gavin's gaze narrowed. "Is there more to the story than what you've told me?"

Immediately, he watched as she put up a wall between them before answering, confirming the belief that she wasn't telling him everything.

"Someone tried to run me off the road earlier and now Uncle Paxton is missing, and they've obviously searched the house. I'd say that's enough proof Paxton stumbled onto something."

Gavin peered around the darkness. She was right. The place had been tossed. Those men had to be looking for something in particular. His guess was they hadn't found it, and so they'd taken Paxton because they believed he knew where it was.

He couldn't imagine what Paxton had gotten himself involved in.

"Why would your uncle ask you to meet him here?" he asked in amazement. "Paxton had to know this would be the first place those men would look for him. Why put your life in jeopardy?"

For this, Jamie had no answer. "I don't know. He must have had his reasons, though. Gavin, I'm worried about him."

Gavin couldn't ease her fears any because he had the same bad feeling in his gut. Chaos surrounding them. It looked like a bomb had gone off. "Are you sure you don't have some idea what Paxton might be involved in?"

She started to say something, but seemed to think better of it. "I don't. I told you everything I know."

Their eyes held. He knew her well. Gavin could see there was more to the story than what she'd told him. She didn't trust him. There was a time when they'd been close. Shared everything. That had ended the day her father killed his.

Jamie slowly got to her feet. She was less than steady, and he grabbed her waist.

"I'm okay." She shook off his help.

"Wait here. Let me take a look around," he told her in an annoyed tone. He was annoyed with her for not trusting him. He was the same Gavin she'd once claimed to love. More than anything, he was angry at the way things had turned out between them and their two families.

He searched the rest of the rooms on one side of the house. When he came back to the living room, she was nowhere in sight.

Fear shot through him. "Jamie!"

She stuck her head out of her dad's old bedroom. "I think Uncle Paxton's in real trouble. You have to see this."

"I told you to stay put." He sounded ticked off because he was. She never did listen to reason. Some things hadn't changed one bit.

He followed her into the room.

"We have to find out who took him before it's too late. Paxton's hurt." She used her phone as a flashlight. The light bounced off a six-by-eight-inch spot on the carpet. It looked like dried blood. The second he saw it, all his anger toward Jamie evaporated.

She was right. Whatever Paxton had become

involved in had landed him in some serious trouble, and Gavin wasn't sure they would be able to find him before it was too late.

THREE

She drew in a frightened breath and racked her brain, trying to recall where she'd recognized that one man's voice from. Yet no matter how hard she tried, the recollection remained elusive.

"We have to find out where they took him before it's too late. If these are the same men who killed your father, they won't hesitate to do the same to Uncle Paxton once they have whatever it is they're looking for." With Paxton's warning not to go to the local authorities, they were on their own and she had no idea where to start.

Was it possible that the sheriff's office was somehow responsible for Charles's death and had covered it up? If that were true, and with Paxton shooting off his mouth around town for years about Noah's innocence, they'd have to find a way to silence him if he'd accidently stumbled onto the truth.

Gavin examined the destroyed house. "I have no idea what's going on, but it's obvious Paxton has gotten himself into some real trouble. When I went into the woods following the light, the man I ran into said he was hunting, but he was lying. When I heard the shot and tried to take him in, he attacked me. Then he and two of his partners got away."

For the first time, Jamie noticed that he was holding his side. "You're hurt." She hurried over and touched his hand, but he grabbed hers and pulled it away.

"I'm okay." His tone held anger.

She stared into his eyes, hurt by his reaction. "What's going on here?"

He blew out a breath. "I wish I knew. Are you sure there's nothing more you and Paxton talked about in the past? Anything that might shed light on how to find him? It doesn't matter how small it may seem."

She wondered how much to tell him about recognizing the man's voice, and what the two had said when they believed she was unconscious. Gavin had expressed doubts before. Did she dare trust him with what she'd overheard? Or would he think she was as paranoid as Paxton? She couldn't face his rejection again.

"Only what I've already told you. Uncle Paxton believed he'd found the evidence that would clear my father's name. He couldn't talk about it on the phone, but told me no matter what happened, I shouldn't talk to the sheriff's office. He begged me to come home. I could hear the fear in his voice." She suppressed a shudder. Paxton wasn't afraid of much. This had gotten her attention right away.

She lifted her shoulders in a shrug. "You know the rest."

Jamie could see that what she said didn't make a lot of sense to a trained law enforcement agent.

"And you're positive they took him?" When she couldn't hide her hurt that he didn't believe her, he added, "Paxton would obviously have expected someone to show up here at some point. Especially if he believed the sheriff's office was involved. Maybe he got wind of what was happening and slipped away before they arrived. Those men could have been trying to trick you into thinking they had your uncle. Maybe see if you would lead them to Paxton."

Jamie didn't believe it. "There was a scuffle. They *had someone*, Gavin. Even if it wasn't Uncle Paxton, they took someone against their will. And Uncle Paxton was here recently. He left his phone behind. I know my uncle. He never goes anywhere without his phone. The man who took it from me said, 'I've got his phone. Let's get *him* out of here.'"

She could see that he still wasn't fully convinced. "Let's not jump to any conclusions just yet. Paxton's smart. He might have heard the accident happening down the mountain and gotten out of here before those men arrived. You know how sound travels up here. If he left in a hurry, he might leave his phone behind."

While that made sense on the surface, Jamie couldn't let go of what the man had said.

Jamie squared her shoulders, ready to argue what she believed was true. "They took him, Gavin. What are we going to do to get him back?"

They faced each other in a silent standoff. She'd find her uncle with or without his help.

Before he could form an answer, a noise outside drew their attention away from the conversation. It sounded like multiple cars heading up the mountainside.

Gavin hurried outdoors with Jamie glued to his side.

"They're coming this way!"

He listened for a second. "You're right. I'd say they're about at my house right now. Go back inside. I'll be right there." He headed for Ava's old truck and got out the shotgun and shells she kept there, while Jamie didn't move.

"Hurry, Jamie. We need to get out of sight before they arrive," he said once he'd reached her side again. She turned on her heel and ran inside, heading for the window.

Gavin slammed the door shut behind them, then locked it.

She could see three sets of headlights flashing through the wooded area near the road. They were almost to the house.

"Do you still remember how to use one of these?" Gavin asked and handed her the shotgun.

"I think so." At one time, she and Gavin had hunted game in the area together. She was an excellent shot. Although it had been years since she'd shot a gun, she was confident she could handle the situation.

The first vehicle rolled to a stop out front, its lights on bright. She and Gavin quickly ducked away from the window. Seconds later, two more cars came to a halt.

"I can't tell how many men there are out there, but I'm guessing it's a bunch." Gavin turned his head and stared at her.

"What do you think they want?" The panic growing inside her made it hard to breathe normally.

He shook his head. "Whatever Paxton started obviously didn't sit well with these guys."

There's nothing here... The men who had run her off the road had been looking for something more than just Paxton.

"This is the sheriff's department. You, inside the house, come outside with your hands up."

She recognized the voice right away. It was the man who ran her off the road.

The name of the deputy played through her memory. Now she knew why that voice had sounded so familiar earlier. She'd grown up with Dan Miller.

He'd been right. They did know each other.

"We're outmanned," Gavin said. "If we stay, we'll be in custody and we'll be of no help to Paxton if that happens."

"Last chance. We know you're in there." A brief silence followed and then the men opened fire. Jamie and Gavin hit the floor at the same time as bullets riddled windows and walls.

"Wait here," Gavin said once the shots had ended. He crept low to the ground and went to her dad's old bedroom. More shots took out the window and sent glass flying. After the noise of broken glass faded, an eerie silence reigned.

"I don't see anyone back behind the house," Gavin said after he returned. "We have to get out of here before we're trapped inside. Just the two of us won't be able to hold them off for long."

What he said was true, but they wouldn't get far on foot. The people outside would eventually storm the house and see it was empty. They'd come looking for Gavin and Jamie.

Gavin crept to the window once more. "They're just sitting there. Almost as if they're waiting for something or someone." He came back to where she was.

"They don't want to bring Uncle Paxton in, they want to kill him," Jamie said.

"I'm not sure they're after Paxton at all," Gavin said. "I think they know *we're* in here."

She stared wide-eyed at him. Was Gavin right?

"Sorry, I know this is hard. Let's get going. Stay as low as possible. We don't know what they have planned for sure, but they could be sending men around behind the house at any moment. At any rate, we don't have much time."

He went to the back door and cracked it, then whispered, "I don't see anyone yet. We have to be as quiet as possible, which is going to be hard, seeing as there's no moon or stars visible through the clouds."

Gavin tucked his weapon behind his back and slung the shotgun over his shoulder before easing out the door. He took her hand. They'd taken only a couple of steps when a board squeaked beneath their feet. Gavin froze. Seconds ticked by, yet the men out front didn't seem to have heard it. They continued to talk amongst themselves.

Gavin pointed to an area straight behind the house where someone had cleared a large part of the property back there.

"We can't afford to go back for the truck," he whispered. "If we head out that direction, we can circle through the woods behind the house until we reach the road again. Once we get to Ava's place, my car is there. We'll have a means to escape. But if Andy is involved in this, then he knows we're together and were heading up here. You have to wonder if these men do as well."

Easing carefully off the porch, together they headed toward the cleared area as fast as they could. It was early autumn in the mountains, yet already the leaves had begun falling, making each step precarious.

Once they reached the top of the hill behind the house, they stopped. Jamie looked behind them. She could still hear the men talking.

"Charge the house." Dan Miller gave the order. Unease balled in her stomach. Uncle Paxton had been right in warning her against contacting the sheriff's office.

"Hurry, Jamie. It won't take them long to realize no one's in the house." Gavin started running and she followed. They couldn't afford to get caught now. Paxton was in real danger. Whatever her uncle had uncovered, these men wanted him dead because of it.

Once they topped another hill, there was no time to rest. They headed down the other side at breakneck speed.

Jamie hadn't been back here in years, but she could see that Paxton had made an effort to clear the entire space out recently. The dirt appeared freshly turned. He'd told her previously that he wanted to start farming the space behind the house. That explained the clearing out, but Paxton wasn't one to stick with a plan for long. Maybe this time was different.

With the recent clearing, the countryside was littered with felled trees that made the going slow. Jamie stopped for a second to gather her breath. From behind them, she could hear the men's voices carrying.

"There's no one inside," one of the men said.

Her gaze shot to Gavin. "They can't have gotten far. Find them," Dan Miller ordered. He was clearly the one calling the shots. Where was Andy Lawson in all this? Was he trying to keep his hands clean?

Gavin grabbed her hand. "We need to hurry."

As they rushed deeper into the woods, Jamie spotted what she at first thought was a fallen log. She stopped.

Gavin reached her side. "What is it?" he asked, glancing behind them.

"There." She pointed to the object, which wasn't anything as innocent as a log. A body lay face down. Someone was dead in the woods.

"Oh, no... Gavin." Her deepest fear was that

it was Paxton. She couldn't look. Jamie didn't want to see her beloved uncle lying dead on the cold, wet ground.

Gavin knew exactly what she was thinking because he thought the same.

Jamie had turned away. She couldn't watch. "Please tell me it's not him," she whispered, almost as if in prayer.

Slowly, Gavin eased the body over. Momentary relief rushed over him. "It's not Paxton," he assured her, but he knew the man lying dead there. And so did Jamie.

She turned. Her hand clapped over her mouth in surprise. "I can't believe it. That's Terry Williams. What happened to him?" she asked in shock.

Terry and Paxton had been good friends for as long as Gavin could remember. Was Terry dead because of something Paxton uncovered? The man had a single gunshot wound in his forehead, assuring Gavin this was no accident. The wound was fresh. There was no doubt this had been the shot he'd heard earlier.

"He's been shot," he told her quietly. "Terry has to be the person those two took from your house."

Tears were in her eyes. "I still can't believe it.

Why would someone want to harm Terry? He's just a kind, gentle soul who's never hurt anyone."

Gavin could think of only one explanation. "This thing is quickly escalating. We have to get off this mountain before we end up like Terry."

"We can't leave him like this." Jamie's voice broke as she looked at the man lying on the ground.

Gavin got to his feet and helped her up. Behind them, he could hear the noise of men making their way through the woods.

"They're coming up pretty fast." Gavin did his best to cover the body with leaves. "That's all we can do for now." He looked into her eyes. "I promise we'll come back for him. We'll give him a proper burial once this is all over."

She slowly nodded. "Which way do we go from here? I'm all turned around."

Gavin tried to regain his bearings. He pointed to the right. If his internal compass was correct, that should take them to his family home.

Several flashlights scanned the area behind them. They were all out of time. "Run, Jamie," he told her.

"There. Up ahead. I see them!" one of the men pursuing them yelled.

"Duck!" Gavin barely got the words out before shots were fired. Bullets flew past them. Jamie dove for the nearest tree, with Gavin close behind her.

They couldn't stand still and wait for the men to capture them. Gavin pointed up ahead. If they could stay behind tree coverage and out of sight as much as possible, they might stand a chance of reaching the house.

He tossed her the shotgun. "Go ahead of me. I'll cover you." She hesitated, not wanting to leave him behind. "It's okay. Hurry, Jamie."

With one final look his way, Jamie turned and headed for the next tree while Gavin opened fire, forcing one of the men to retreat.

When there was a lull in the firefight, Gavin dashed after Jamie. The men must have seen the movement because they started shooting again.

Gavin flattened against another tree and edged out just enough to fire.

The air was thick with gun smoke. When a tenuous silence reclaimed the area, Gavin ran as fast as he could. He'd almost reached Jamie when more rounds exploded around him. One hit its mark.

Gavin yelled out in pain as the bullet seared into his left side. He almost lost his footing; his hand touched the ground as he stumbled several times, but managed to keep from falling. It was imperative that he stay mobile and keep moving.

Once he was stable, he held on to his wounded side as blood seeped through his clothes.

Jamie had turned at the sound of his scream.

"Don't stop!" he yelled and waved her off when she started for him. They had to keep going.

It felt as if they'd been running for hours. Ignoring the pain and the faintness, Gavin hit the road just a little behind Jamie. The world around him spun and his stomach heaved as he came close to passing out. They were almost to Jamie's downed car. Just a little bit farther to Ava's place. He just had to hang on.

Jamie hurried to his side.

"We need to get out of sight before they catch up." He pointed to the wooded area on the opposite side of the road. In his condition, it might as well be on the other side of the moon. He wasn't sure he could make it another foot.

Blood soaked his hand, and his vision blurred. It was a struggle to keep from losing consciousness. He blinked hard and forced back the nausea.

Jamie grabbed him around the waist and together they left the woods. Crossing the road meant they were out in the open and exposed.

His breathing became more labored. They reached the opposite side of the road and Gavin was thankful for the cover of trees. He needed to rest.

"No, we can't stop. We have to keep moving. It's not much farther to Ava's," Jamie told him, yet putting one foot in front of the other was a near-impossible task. He leaned heavily against her, losing track of time. How long had they been out here?

"There it is," Jamie exclaimed and he forced himself to focus.

The light he'd left on in the kitchen came into view. He almost lost hope. From where he stood it seemed miles away, and he wasn't sure he had the strength to make it to the light.

Behind them, he could hear their pursuers. They'd reached the road.

"Go ahead of me. Get to the house. Call the state police." His words slurred. He couldn't hang on much longer.

Jamie ignored what he said. She kept her arm around his waist and helped him along as best she could. He winced in pain, his strength slowly ebbing away. They had to reach the house. It was their only chance. If he passed out now, it was all over.

With each step jarring through his injured body, they made it to the edge of Ava's property.

"We're almost there, Gavin. Hang on a little

bit longer. Please, just hang on." He barely registered the desperation in Jamie's voice.

He thought he managed a weak nod, but wasn't sure if it was real or a hallucination. The house came into view. Almost there. The steps leading up to the porch loomed in front of him like an insurmountable fortress forcing him to stop long enough to catch his breath.

"Come on, Gavin. We can't stop now. We're almost there. Just one step at a time."

Perspiration beaded his forehead. He pulled himself up onto the first step and pain shot through his side. He squeezed his eyes closed, fighting back bile.

The next step was just as difficult, as were the rest. Once they reached the porch, he struggled and somehow managed to take out the key, yet he couldn't hold it steady enough to open the door.

"Here, let me." Jamie took the key from his unresisting hand and slipped it into the lock.

The world around him became fuzzy. Gavin collapsed against Jamie, his full weight almost bringing her to her knees. He had no idea how she managed to keep them both upright.

"Hang on, Gavin," Jamie said, sounding out of breath. She pushed the door open. His grandmother's living room flashed before his eyes. It was the same view he had every single time he entered the familiar room. He was coming home.

He mumbled something unintelligible.

"What did you say?" Jamie asked, clearly not understanding. He had no idea, either. The sight in front of him brought tears to his eyes. He loved this old house. Had loved the woman who owned it more than anything. He couldn't imagine not calling this place home ever again.

"Home." The word was barely distinguishable. It would never be home again. Not without Ava.

"Yes, we're home." Jamie obviously hadn't understood what he meant, and he was too weak to try to explain it.

She put both arms around his waist and all but dragged him over to the sofa, stopping long enough to catch her breath. She was a slender thing. He couldn't imagine how difficult it was for her to haul his six-foot-plus frame from the door to the sofa.

Gavin groaned as pain shot up his side when Jamie managed to lower his wounded body.

Each breath he took hurt like crazy. His shirt was wet with his own blood.

He closed his eyes and tried to gather enough breath into his body. When he opened them again, he saw Jamie hurrying back over to the door. The darkness outside disappeared when she slammed it closed and relocked it, sliding the custom-made locking system his grandmother had installed back into place.

Ava. He'd buried his grandmother today. Gavin couldn't get the image of her lying in that coffin out of his head. Tears gathered in his eyes again. He slumped down onto the sofa, his world turned sideways. He was barely aware of Jamie saying his name before his eyes drifted shut and everything, including her, vanished completely.

FOUR

"Gavin!" Jamie screamed and ran to his side. He'd slumped down against the sofa seat, his eyes closed. "Gavin." He still didn't respond.

Jamie jerked his jacket open and recoiled at the muddy red spot covering his shirt where blood had soaked through. Gavin was in real trouble, and she had no idea how to help him.

"Stay with me, Gavin." She shook him gently. His eyes barely opened. He mumbled something she didn't catch before his eyes dropped shut again.

"Gavin, wake up. I need you. Please, wake up." She shook him harder. It took several tries before he finally roused.

Confused, he stared up at her for the longest time, as if he didn't know what was going on. Her fear must have registered through the disorientation. He reached up and touched her cheek gently. "Don't worry, Jamie. It's going to be okay."

His words were still slurred and he winced. The simple effort of speaking was difficult.

Gavin drew in several shallow breaths then tried to sit up. He clutched his side, pain etched on his face before he slumped back against the sofa.

"Gavin, you've been shot. What do I do? How can I help you?" Her voice shook. His pain scared the daylights out of her. The thought of losing him like this was terrifying.

"Check the security system. The monitor is on the desk. We need to see if they followed us here," he forced out.

Jamie hurried to Ava's old desk and clicked on the monitor. Five different angles of the property came into view. What she saw there was terrifying. Armed men dressed in sheriff's uniforms were easing toward the house.

"They're here, Gavin." As she watched, three of the men cleared the front porch. Miller was one of them.

"We know you're in there. Come out with your hands up," Miller ordered.

Jamie turned toward Gavin who held his finger up to his lips.

"Break the door down," Miller told one of his men.

The man slammed his shoulder against the door, but it didn't budge. They didn't know the advanced security measures Ava had put into place. Steel reinforced doors, with state-of-the-art locking systems on all windows and doors. The place was a virtual fortress. When Ava had first told her about the security upgrade, Jamie couldn't imagine what the woman was expecting to happen. Now, she was grateful that Ava had taken such extreme precautions.

After several more tries without avail, Miller's phone rang and he answered it, speaking briefly to someone. "He needs us back there. Let's go. They're not going anywhere. Not in his condition."

Jamie watched the men leave the way they came, her hands shaking.

She went back to Gavin. "We have to get you out of here before they come back. You need to be checked out at the hospital." He was fading fast.

"We can't. They'll be checking all the hospitals. You're going to have to dress the wound yourself," he murmured.

Wide-eyed, she stared down at him. "I might hurt you."

He grabbed her hand, forcing her to be still. "There's no one else who can help me. It has to be you. You can do this."

Dread wrapped its slithery arms around her. Gavin was right. She was all he had, and she would do everything in her power to take care of him.

"You're right. I can," she murmured without really feeling confident that she could.

As she stared into his eyes, unwelcome feelings resurfaced. She'd spent years trying to deny it, but that didn't change the truth. She still cared for Gavin and couldn't bear it if something bad happened to him.

"Thank you." He managed a smile, and tears filled her eyes. She didn't want to lose him.

Hugging him close, she was careful not to hurt him more. When she would have pulled away, he cupped her face. "Thank you, Jamie."

Theirs had been a love story that had ended with two broken hearts. Now they were facing a life-and-death situation in which the outcome was unpredictable. There were no guarantees they'd survive to find Paxton, whether dead or alive.

He let her go and drew in several labored breaths while Jamie prayed for strength.

"You need something to sanitize the wound and some dry bandages." His voice was barely audible, the injury draining his strength.

"Okay. I'll get them."

He smiled at her attempt at bravery. "That's my girl. You have to be quick, though. We don't know how much time we have."

She got to her feet, went to the master bathroom, and she grabbed alcohol and a towel to help with the bleeding. The medicine chest contained only a box of Band-Aids. She'd need something much bigger to wrap the wound up securely. In the hallway linen closet, she found fresh sheets. Ava always kept them available in case someone dropped by for a visit and decided to stay.

Jamie ripped one of the sheets into strips that would serve as bandages. Once she had everything she needed, she went back to Gavin. His eyes were closed again and he was so still.

Dropping the supplies, she hurried to his side, kneeling next to the sofa. "Gavin!"

He slowly opened his eyes, saw all the worry on her face and did his best to reassure her. "I'm okay, I was just resting. Are you ready?"

She wasn't anywhere close, but Gavin needed her to be strong, and she'd do anything for him. "Yes, I'm ready."

Sitting down next to him, she slowly unbuttoned his shirt. The wound was a bloody mess. The effort of pulling his shirt free left him drained of energy. She couldn't imagine how difficult it was going to be dressing the wound.

Jamie didn't realize he was watching her, no doubt seeing all her fears, until he spoke. "I'll be okay. I'm tough," he assured her.

She gently wiped the area around the wound clear of blood, then cleaned it with the alcohol. He cringed as the medicine hit the wound and stung. One hand gripped the side of the sofa.

Once she'd finished cleaning the spot, Gavin slumped back against the sofa, exhausted.

"We're almost done," she said gently, then folded some of the bandages and placed them over the wound.

"You'll need to apply pressure until the bleeding stops." Gavin forced the words out through clenched teeth.

Blood still oozed from the wound. Jamie placed her hands over the bandage and pressed hard. Gavin squeezed his eyes shut and bit his bottom lip.

"I'm sorry," she whispered, hating that she was the one to cause him pain. "I know it hurts."

It felt as if it took forever before the bleeding finally subsided. After removing the bloodied bandage, she put a clean one in its place, then took several strips of cloth and eased them around his waist until the wound was secured.

When Gavin lay back against the sofa, Jamie hurried to the kitchen and brought a glass of water over. She sat back down. "Here, take a sip."

She held his head up so that he could drink. He managed a single swallow then collapsed again.

"I'm not sure what to do next," she said. With Gavin so weak, they couldn't leave the house. They wouldn't get very far. If Miller and his men showed up again, would they find a way inside?

He didn't answer, and she shook him once more. Gavin didn't respond. Fear gripped her and Jamie grabbed his wrist, feeling for a pulse. It was there, weak but steady.

Jamie leaned back against the sofa. What if Gavin didn't wake up? What if the men showed up again? When her fear threatened to take control, she hit her knees and prayed.

"We need Your help. Please make him better."

Still kneeling close to Gavin's side, she watched him closely. Although he still hadn't moved and he was so pale, he seemed to be resting more comfortably, which was probably the best thing for him right now. Would they be able to stay hidden long enough for him to recover his strength?

Jamie got to her feet and killed the lights, then went over to the window. Nothing could be seen through the darkness. Feeling helpless, she let the curtain drop and went back to check on Gavin. He was sleeping peacefully. She took one of Ava's quilts from the closet and placed it over him for warmth.

Laying the shotgun on the coffee table, she

took the Glock that Gavin had tucked close to him and shoved it into her jacket pocket.

It had been years since she'd been to Ava's home. Probably the last time had been when she was a teenager. While most things still looked the same, there were some significant differences.

She'd noticed the first when she'd locked the door. The locking system was like nothing she'd ever seen before. Even though Ava had told her she was putting in the security measures, Jamie still couldn't reconcile it with the strong but sweet woman she'd known for so many years. What was Ava expecting to happen to her that she needed such sophisticated protection?

In several of their conversations after Jamie first left the area, Ava had told her about how heroin had the county of Darlan in a stranglehold. Had Ava been afraid of someone breaking into her home and stealing from her to support their habit?

Jamie couldn't help but wonder if what was happening to her and Gavin was in some way related to the drug problem in Darlan. Was that what Uncle Paxton was trying to warn her about? If so, then how did the heroin connect to the sheriff's office or to a ten-year-old murder? There had to be a connection.

An uneasy thought made her shiver. Ava Dalton had made it clear to anyone who would listen throughout the years that she didn't believe Noah had killed her son. Was her death really due to a heart attack, like the coroner claimed, or because someone wanted to silence her, as well?

While she tried to make sense of the impossible, the monitor on Ava's desk suddenly flashed on, giving views of every part of the property. Someone was here. Jamie hurried over to the screen and studied it. What had triggered the sensors? Then she saw it. Several of the same armed men from earlier were making their way through the woods behind the house.

Horrified, she watched as the men methodically marched across the yard. Once they reached the house, they stopped and then unexpectedly left the property.

They were looking for something in particular. Why hadn't they returned to the house? Were they standing back, waiting for her and Gavin to emerge so that they could arrest them...or worse?

Jamie went back over to where Gavin still rested peacefully. As much as she wanted to wake him up and tell him what had just happened, she knew rest was the best medicine for him now.

With nothing else to do but wait, Jamie went into the kitchen. She needed something to do.

Without turning on any lights, she made coffee. When she'd woken that morning, the only thing on her mind had been defending her client, who was down to his last appeal. And then Uncle Paxton had called, and her life in Louisville had taken second place to her only living relative. She'd managed to get Adam Sullivan's upcoming trial extended for another week. She prayed it would be long enough to save her uncle.

Now, exhausted beyond belief, Jamie was afraid to let her guard down for a second. She'd watch over Gavin until he was stronger. No matter what, she wouldn't let him down.

With coffee in hand, she went over to the monitor. Nothing stirred outside. Had the men truly moved on in their search, or were they still out there somewhere, waiting for them to come out into the open before they'd attack?

Gavin's eyes felt glued shut. It was a struggle to force them open. Where was he? It took a moment before he remembered what had happened. Jamie being run off the road. The race through the woods that resulted in his being shot. The desperate trek to his grandmother's house. He was home. The room was dark. Where was Jamie? The only light was coming from somewhere behind him.

It took all his strength to make it to a sitting position. Breathing was a struggle.

Someone hurried his way. Jamie! She was safe. He could see the concern on her face. Had something happened?

"Don't try to move. You're still very weak." The gentleness in her tone matched her eyes.

"How long have I been out?" he managed in a barely audible voice. His side hurt like crazy, and he felt as weak as a kitten.

"Several hours. You lost a lot of blood, Gavin."

He knew she was worried about him, but there was an edge to her voice that had him concerned. "Something else happened while I was out." It wasn't a question.

She sat next to him. "Yes. Not too long after you passed out, your grandmother's security system went crazy. Several of the same armed men from earlier made their way through the woods behind the house. They searched the yard as if they were looking for something, yet once they reached the house, they stopped and then unexpectedly left the property. It was…strange."

Gavin shook his head. "I have no idea what they could be looking for."

"Me either, but I don't think we can afford to stay here much longer."

She was right. Miller would want to take both him and Jamie in for questioning. He'd try to find a way to silence them. Gavin couldn't let that happen. Paxton had stumbled onto something big that definitely involved the sheriff's office, and he and Jamie were outnumbered. Miller and his men would keep coming after them. Using their badges, they'd be unstoppable.

"How often do you and your uncle talk?" he asked, the question taking her by surprise.

"Maybe once a week, sometimes more, depending on our schedules. Why do you ask?"

Because I'm desperate. Because I'm afraid I can't keep us safe, was on the tip of his tongue, but he couldn't voice his fears aloud. Jamie was counting on him.

"I'm just thinking Paxton might have said something in passing that didn't make sense at the time, but in the light of what's happened tonight, might be helpful in finding him."

Gavin could see her replaying their previous conversation over in her head. "Paxton told me he was closing down the coal mine for a while to do some repairs. At the time, I didn't think anything of it, but the last time I spoke to him, he told me that the mine was still closed." She stopped to look at him. "He was barely making a living as it was. There was no way he could afford to have the mine closed for so long. I'm wondering if maybe he was doing more than mining down there."

Since Gavin's father's murder and Noah's incarceration, prior to passing away, the mine that the two friends had worked together for years had been sitting mostly untouched. With Charles's death, controlling interest had gone to Ava. She'd let Paxton mine it as he saw fit. Ava had told Gavin occasionally that while Paxton and his friend Terry Williams worked the mine, they'd never found the mother lode that Noah and Charles believed existed beneath the mountain.

"Ava mentioned on several occasions how the use of the drug heroin had gotten really bad in Darlan. I remember her talking about it when I first left Darlan ten years ago. Do you think this has something to do with drug trafficking?"

He managed a nod. "Possibly. You think Paxton could be hiding whatever Miller and his men are looking for at the mine?" Gavin asked, then considered the possibility. It made sense in a way. That would explain why he wasn't mining. "Does anyone besides you know about the repairs?"

She shook her head. "Not as far as I know."

Even if Paxton hadn't discussed the repairs with anyone, the mine would be the first place Miller would look after he checked Paxton's house. There were no guarantees they'd find him there alive. Still, they had to try, because right now, they had no idea why the sheriff's office was willing to kill the older man.

"We need to get to the Darlan Mountain Mine as soon as possible." He grabbed the sofa arm and tried to stand. His knees threatened to buckle, and the world swam before his eyes. Gavin sank back down. He'd never felt so weak before. How on earth was he going to protect them, should something happen?

"You need to rest," Jamie insisted. "You were shot. You've suffered a tremendous blow to your system."

He closed his eyes until the world settled down. "There's no time. We need to get out of here while we still can. Miller and his men could return at any moment."

"At least let me change your bandage, and then I'll make you something to eat. It'll give you energy."

As much as he wanted to get to the mine as fast as possible, Jamie was right. He needed something to boost his strength.

He watched as she skillfully removed the bandage and treated the wound before wrapping it again. While the spot was still red and swollen, at least the bleeding had stopped.

Jamie gathered the used bandages and got to her feet. Before she could walk away, he clasped her hand, holding her there. She looked down at him with uncertainty written on her face.

"Thank you," he murmured with an attempt at a smile, while wanting to say so much more. He still cared for her, and he couldn't think of anyone he'd rather have on his side.

She returned his smile. "I didn't do anything you wouldn't have done for me."

"Maybe, but still, thank you."

She squeezed his hand and then stepped back. "You're welcome." He watched as she hurried away, and he tried to get his chaotic heartbeat under control. Feelings still existed between them, but he'd made so many mistakes with Jamie. Now they were facing a life-and-death situation, and he was injured. Could he keep them safe?

Gavin slowly struggled to his feet and followed her to the kitchen. She caught him coming her way and hurried to his side.

"You need to lie back down."

He shook his head. "I need to get back on my feet as soon as possible. Moving around will help."

Resigned, she shrugged and handed him some coffee. He accepted it gratefully and took a sip. He'd forgotten how refreshing a simple cup of coffee could be.

"There doesn't appear to be much in your grandmother's fridge besides eggs and bacon."

To Gavin it sounded like a feast. "Sounds good to me." Slowly, he lowered himself down to one of the stools in front of the bar. Trying to hide his exhaustion from her was impossible, yet there was nothing that could be done about it. Although being shot had taken its toll, the fast-paced life he led as a spy was catching up with him, as well. He'd been burning the candle at both ends for years. He'd been in Kandahar when he'd learned about his grandmother's passing. He'd caught the first flight home to Darlan.

Even though he'd been home for almost a week, Gavin had barely spent any time at Ava's house. Too many bittersweet memories were stored up here. All the Christmases he and his father would go out to the woods and cut down a tree for his grandmother. Ava always wanted the biggest tree they could find. The Easter egg hunts as a child. He could picture Ava in just about every square inch of the homestead. Even after witnessing his grandmother's body being lowered into the ground, Gavin still couldn't imagine death conquering her.

Jamie set a plate of bacon and eggs in front of him, then touched his hand. "I miss her, too. I still can't believe she's gone."

Gavin swallowed emotions that he wasn't

ready to deal with just yet. "Yeah, I can still see her standing where you are, making all those amazing meals she used to put together as if it were nothing at all. Especially during the holidays."

Jamie smiled, reminiscing. "I remember that one Christmas when we all got together over here. That was a great day."

He remembered the time she mentioned, too. He and Jamie hadn't yet started dating, but he'd known he was crazy about her, even back then. Every time he'd looked at her, his young heart had gone crazy.

"Your grandmother told me you went to work for the CIA. She was proud of you."

There was much more that she wasn't saying, but he wasn't surprised that she and Ava had talked. His grandmother was always dropping hints about their conversations whenever she spoke to Gavin. Ava had always adored Jamie.

He nodded. "After my father's death, I stopped believing in anything good. I joined the CIA and then later…got married." He slid her a look. She was clearly surprised. "I became driven by my career for a long time, and because of it, my marriage collapsed around me. Emily deserved better than what I could give her."

Gavin watched as Jamie processed what he'd said. Was it just wishful thinking on his part, or did she actually seem unhappy about what he'd told her?

"I had no idea you were married. Ava never mentioned it." She swallowed visibly. "I'm sorry it didn't work out, but I understand about failed relationships. I haven't been able to keep anything together long enough to even be called a relationship."

He smiled at her admission. "I knew I had to do something to redeem myself. When I was offered a job with the Scorpion team, I finally found my purpose. I love the men and women on the team, and it was through my comrades that I came to know God. He changed my life. Gave me a purpose. Now, I can't imagine my life without God in it."

Jamie returned his smile. "I'm happy for you. I know the importance of faith in my own life. It's proven itself so many times in the past."

She took her plate over to the bar and sat next to him. "Why do you think they took his phone?" she asked, her forehead knitted together into a frown.

Gavin put down his fork. "They were probably trying to find out who he spoke to recently. Maybe track his movements." He stopped and shrugged.

Without Paxton, all their questions would remain unanswered.

"I just hope he's okay," she said, and he could hear the concern in her voice.

He swiveled to face her. "Paxton's a tough old guy. He'll be okay." He tried to reassure her while hoping he hadn't lied, because he had a bad feeling. Something was terribly wrong in Darlan.

Gavin finished his meal and struggled to his feet, intent on washing off his plate.

"Here, let me do that." Jamie took both plates over to the sink and rinsed them off while Gavin eased around the great room, hoping to regain some of his strength.

"I have some pain medicine in my bag, along with some antibiotics. I'll just go get it."

She watched him leave with a worried look on her face. She was probably wondering how they were going to make it out of this thing alive in the condition he was in.

Once he found the medicine, he took the correct dosage and went back to where Jamie had finished clearing away their breakfast. Outside, it was just getting light.

Jamie glanced out at the breaking dawn. "Why would they kill Terry? He's the sweetest guy. He'd never hurt anyone."

Growing up, Terry Williams had been part of Gavin's life every bit as much as Paxton had. Terry and Paxton had been friends for as long as

Gavin could remember. Terry grew up a miner and proud of it, but he was also one of the nicest men Gavin had ever known. He remembered how, after his father's death, Terry had stopped by pretty much every day to check on him and Ava.

He shook her head. He didn't want to tell her, but the only explanation was that Terry had been killed because of his relationship to Paxton. Someone thought Terry knew something important.

Gavin slowly went over to the monitor and checked the cameras outside. "I don't see anyone. We should probably take this opportunity and get out of here while we still can. I'm going to gather some things we might need along the way."

He went back to the room he'd used as a child and grabbed his backpack, filling it with supplies—extra bandages and medicine, a flashlight and a lighter. His backup weapon and ammo for the Glock and the shotgun, along with a knife and rope. Useful things to have when entering a mine.

Doing the simplest of things was difficult. He had to stop periodically to regain his strength. If they had to fight their way out of a situation, he wasn't so sure he would survive it.

"We'll have to take my rental car," Gavin told her when he came back to the living room.

With his grandmother's old truck still in the woods near Jamie's home, they'd have no choice. But the path to the mine was a rough one, especially coming up the back way like they'd be doing. They wouldn't be able to make it the full way up by car.

Jamie didn't seem nearly as confident about what they would be forced to do. "Gavin, you've lost a lot of blood. I don't think you're up to the challenge of walking the rest of the way to the mine."

He could see she was worried about him. She came over to where he stood and gently touched his arm. "Let me check out the mine on my own."

Gavin understood her fears, but there was no way he was going to let her go down there alone.

He shook his head. "It's too dangerous. We don't know what we'll find once we're in the mine." And he couldn't stand the thought of anything happening to her.

"Gavin…" She bit back whatever else she'd been about to say before giving in. "Fine."

"As soon as it gets light, we'll head out. Hopefully, those guys will have moved on."

As the world outside grew light, he prayed for

the strength to keep them safe. Because right now, he wasn't nearly as convinced they'd walk out of this thing alive.

the sponge to keep them clear. He had s
now, however, figured it out because they'd walk
out of the hiding spot

FIVE

Just making it out to the car drained Gavin's energy at an alarming rate. Jamie took the backpack from him and put it in the back seat, then
hit the garage door opener and the door slowly
slid open.

"You'll have to drive. I don't trust myself behind the wheel." His voice was little more than
a whisper. Jamie was frightened for him. If they
were attacked, could she protect him?

Once she'd helped him get his six-foot-plus
frame inside the compact's passenger seat, Jamie
rounded the back of the car and glanced around
the filmy light of a new day. So far, there didn't
appear to be anyone around. Where had Miller
and his men gone?

Jamie got behind the wheel and backed out
of the garage. Gavin tucked his Glock beneath
his seat. The shotgun was hidden behind the
back seat.

"Ready?" she asked. The tiniest of nods did

little to clear away her concerns. She eased down the long drive pitted with potholes. Ava and her husband, Henry, had built the house close to the edge of their property when they were first married. Ava had told her that the spot where the house sat was the first place she and her husband had kissed. It was a sweet story that had stuck with Jamie through the years. Tough as nails, Ava had also had a gentle side that very few people other than family and close friends ever got to see. It was what had made her so special. Jamie fought back tears at the memory.

As much as she didn't want to give in to her fears, Jamie couldn't help but worry about her uncle's safety. She believed if Paxton had been able to reach out to her, he would have by now. The Darlan Mountain Mine was the only logical place where Uncle Paxton would go to hide out. It was his second home—though anyone who knew him would realize this. Would they be too late?

Jamie stopped when she reached the road, her hands sweaty on the wheel. Once she was positive no one was coming, she pulled onto the mountain road and headed back toward her family home. Her thoughts returned to the frightening events of the previous night right here on the mountain. Dan Miller, the man whose voice she'd recognized from the past, someone sworn to serve and protect, had tried to run her off the road.

Their car barely made it out of the drive before a deputy sheriff's SUV appeared behind them, seemingly from nowhere, flashing its lights. With the previous night's encounter still fresh in her mind, Jamie stared at the rearview mirror in horror. "That looks like the same sheriff's deputy who came to my house last night. He's the one who ran me off the road."

Gavin sat up straighter in his seat and squinted behind them. "We need to pull over. We don't want to give him any reason to arrest us. Find a wide spot and stop. Maybe we can find out what he knows."

It was the last thing she wanted to do, but Gavin was right. If they ran, they'd look guilty.

Jamie eased as far off the road as the narrow shoulder would allow. There was no doubt in her mind that Miller had ordered Terry's murder. If he was capable of doing such a senseless thing, he wouldn't hesitate to silence them if he saw them as a threat.

Gavin covered her hand on the wheel. "Try to relax. We don't want to tip him off that something is wrong."

She stared into his eyes, saw the strength she'd always been able to lean on in the past, and slowly nodded.

Miller got out of the SUV and made his way over to the car. With a quick prayer for their safety running through her head, Jamie lowered the window.

The deputy's gaze went from Jamie to Gavin, recognizing them both.

"I'm surprised to see the two of you together again. What are you up to so early this morning?" The suspicion in Miller's voice made it clear he was on alert.

Jamie did her best to sound confident. "I ran into Gavin, and we started reminiscing about when we were younger, growing up here on the mountain. I guess we lost track of time. I'm just heading up to my house now."

She found it strange that Miller didn't ask about her car. Did he suspect she knew it was him who'd run her off the road?

"Have you seen Paxton lately?" he asked with an edge to his tone.

It took everything inside of her not to look away. "No, I haven't. Why do you need him?"

"Because we found Terry Williams's body in the woods behind your place last night. We believe Paxton may have murdered his friend."

The allegation struck her like a blow. Miller was trying to frame Paxton for Terry's murder. "That can't be true. Uncle Paxton would never hurt Terry. They've been friends since they were kids."

Miller wasn't moved by her defense of her uncle. "That may be, but it doesn't change the fact that Terry was found on your property. And people do strange things when their livelihood is threatened."

Fear froze her expression. "What are you talking about?"

Miller smiled smugly. "I'm thinking Terry was going to turn Paxton in for trafficking heroin. Paxton had to get rid of him quickly before that happened. And now Paxton has disappeared, which certainly makes him appear guilty. We know this because we went to your house last night and he wasn't there. Someone else was, though."

Miller's unwavering gaze held hers. Jamie ignored the reference to them being at the house. "Uncle Paxton didn't do what you're accusing him of. He's in Jamesville."

Miller clearly didn't believe her, but for the moment he had nothing to hold them on. "You can be sure I'll check on that. You'd better hope he's there. In the meantime, if you talk to him, tell him to turn himself in. We wouldn't want anything bad to…happen to him if he tried to flee."

Her eyes widened at the threat.

With a final tap on the side of the car, Miller made his way back to his vehicle.

Jamie put the window up with trembling fingers. "What do we do now?" She turned to Gavin.

He peered in the side mirror. "We can't go to the mine, that's for sure. Not with him watching us. Let's head up to your place for now. See if he follows."

Jamie eased the car back onto the road and headed up the mountain. A quick check in the rearview mirror confirmed her worst fear. "He's still coming. Miller's not letting us out of his sight. I can't believe they're trying to frame Uncle Paxton for Terry's death when they're the ones who killed him." She shook her head. "We can't let that happen."

Gavin continued watching as the deputy kept his distance, making it clear he was following them. "We'll do everything we can to keep Paxton safe. But first, we have to find him before they do."

Jamie did her best to keep her speed steady. She couldn't believe what had happened since she'd been home. Less than twenty-four hours ago, her biggest concern had been freeing a wrongfully accused man. Now she and Gavin were trying to stay out of jail long enough themselves to find her uncle, before Miller and his goons took care of whatever problem he posed.

As Jamie rolled to a stop in front of her place, Gavin surveyed the house and surrounding mountainside. The sheriff's department didn't have deputies stationed around. They weren't expecting Paxton to return. Why? He noticed Miller stop a little way down, concealed by a group of trees. "We still have our tail. Let's hope he gets bored after a while and leaves us alone, because if he doesn't, there's no way we can go to the mine. We'd be leading him straight to Paxton, assuming he's hiding there."

Jamie was staring at the spot where he'd left his truck. "Gavin, your truck's gone."

He craned his neck behind them. Miller and his men had moved Ava's truck "I have no idea what's going on here, but I sure don't like it. Let's get inside and out of sight."

He grabbed the backpack filled with supplies and got out of the car, followed by Jamie, and hurried up the steps to the house. The front door was blocked by crime-scene tape.

"What should we do?" She glanced up at him, her eyes filled with worry.

"We go inside. This is your home, and Miller didn't try to stop us when we told him what we were doing." Gavin ripped the tape away from the door and opened it. Jamie hesitated a second, then went inside with a final look at the deputy.

In the light of day, the damage done there was even more alarming than what he'd seen the night before. The destruction left from the hail of bullets was shocking. Shattered glass was everywhere. Broken knickknacks littered the floor of the great room. Furniture was riddled with bullets. Gavin recalled the bloodstains in the bedroom. Someone was injured here. Gavin was positive Terry had been shot where they'd found his body. So whose blood was this? The only explanation was that it had to be Paxton's. The bloodstain didn't appear big enough to be fatal. Maybe he'd been injured by Miller and his men and managed to escape. That would explain why they were still looking for Paxton.

Jamie peeked out the window. "He's not leaving. We can't risk going to the mine and leading him to Paxton."

Gavin joined her by the window. "We won't be able to drive there. We'll have to go on foot. For the time being, we'll stay here. See if he leaves. If not, then we'll have to go back to Ava's and head out after dark."

He looked into her eyes and saw the fear she couldn't hide. Everything inside of him wanted to protect her, but he had to know what they were facing, and Jamie was still holding something back. "I need you to tell me what you haven't yet. Paxton's life might depend on it. You said Miller ran you off the road last night. Are you sure?"

She stared at him for the longest time, evidently surprised, then blew out a sigh, her voice little more than a whisper. "I'm positive. I recognized his voice." She turned to face him fully. It was time to tell him everything. She could trust Gavin. He'd risked his life for her. "He was with someone. They were looking for something in particular. They searched the trunk. The other man said, 'We'd better find him and the stuff before they arrive.'" She shivered, recalling the conversation. "But what was the most frightening was what the other man said next. He said, 'We don't need the hassle of covering up another murder.'" She looked into Gavin's eyes and said, "I think they were talking about your father's murder."

Startled, he couldn't let himself believe what she was saying. Sure the man's words were disturbing, but he wasn't ready to make that leap just yet. "We don't know that. It could mean anything." The hurt on her face was hard to take. She would never give up on proving her father's innocence.

"What do you think they were looking for?" he asked gently, needing to steer the conversation back to safer ground.

She blew out a sigh. "I have no idea, but whatever it is, they're willing to kill for it."

As he looked around the place in the light of day, he saw things that he hadn't earlier. The rooms had been ransacked, but the house looked as if it hadn't been lived in for quite some time.

"Was Paxton still living here?" Gavin asked.

She obviously found the question odd. "As far as I know, yes. Why?" She looked around and saw what he had.

Jamie tried the lights once more. "The electricity was off last night as well. I thought maybe those men had turned it off." She went over to the desk and rummaged around. "There are several months' worth of electricity bills here. The power has been shut off."

"Paxton obviously hasn't been living here in a while. But if he's not staying here, then where?" Their gazes locked.

"The mine. That's the only explanation. The only place where he'd feel safe," Jamie insisted.

She began roaming the small living space where she'd grown up. He wondered if being with him again had brought up any unresolved feelings for her. It certainly had for him.

He'd practically grown up in this house, as well. Even before he and Jamie started dating, the two families had spent a great deal of time together. He remembered Sunday meals here with Noah praying over the food. Noah was like a second father to him, which made what he did that much harder to accept.

Gavin swallowed regret and searched for something to say to fill the awkward silence. He left his spot by the window and sat down on the dusty sofa, the injury drawing down his strength.

"Ava told me you'd become a criminal defense attorney." Jamie shot him a surprised look, and he smiled. "We talked a lot about you," he said in answer to her unasked question. "She was proud of the work you did. She said you were trying to help those who couldn't help themselves…like your father." The last part was difficult to say.

Jamie looked away. He couldn't tell what she was thinking.

There was something he needed to say. "I never told you how sorry I was to hear about Noah's passing, but I was. In spite of everything that happened, he was still like family, and I hated thinking about him in that place. Hated that he passed away there."

Jamie cleared her throat. "Thank you," she murmured, her voice unsteady. "I had no idea when I chose this career path how many cases there were of people being wrongfully incarcerated. It's heartbreaking." She told him about an elderly man by the name of Adam Sullivan whose case was similar to her father's. As she spoke, he could see tears glistening in her eyes. Her passion for her work was obvious.

He slowly got to his feet and went over to where she stood. He took her hand and held it. "I'm sorry," he managed and wished he could erase the ugly past for them both.

After a moment, she nodded and squeezed his hand, then moved away, wiping tears from her face. "It's okay. I love the type of work I do, but it can be emotionally exhausting."

Jamie went back to the window and looked out. "He's still there." She turned back to him. "I don't think he's leaving."

"There's no need to hang around here any longer. Let's head back to Ava's. I just hope we can make it until nightfall without Miller trying something."

He could see the thought was terrifying, and he tried to reassure her.

"Why don't you grab some personal things? If Miller stops us and asks why we were here, you can tell him you came to pick up a few things before heading back to Louisville."

While Jamie looked around the place, Gavin watched Miller's vehicle. If the deputy stopped them, and Gavin was certain that would happen, he would search the car looking for anything that might give him the location where Paxton was hiding. His backup weapon and extra ammo for the Glock and the shotgun, along with a knife and rope might give away too much.

Gavin quickly found a safe place to store them. They could stop back by the house to retrieve the items before heading to the mine.

He moved the bookcase enough so that he could stuff the things behind it and prayed Miller wouldn't grow suspicious and search the house again. He shoved the medicines and extra bandages in his jacket pocket.

"What are you doing?" Jamie asked when she spotted him kneeling near the bookcase. She held a collection of trinkets in her hand.

He straightened awkwardly. His injury made everything more difficult. "It wouldn't do for Miller to find those things in the backpack, and I'm pretty sure he saw it in the back seat. I can't leave it here. He'll wonder where it is." He held the now empty bag open, and she placed the few items inside.

"There's nothing we can do for Paxton right now. Let's get out of here."

With one final look around, Jamie opened the door and stepped out into the foggy morning. Gavin followed her out to the car.

"He'll stop us. Once we're on the road again, he'll stop us and search the car and the bag. Try to appear as calm as you can."

Jamie got behind the wheel once more and started the car, glancing his way. He couldn't begin to hide the toll his injury had taken on his body. He was barely hanging on.

"Gavin, are you okay?" The worry in her voice confirmed how bad he must look.

He managed a nod and tried to sit up straighter. "I'll be fine. I just need to get back to the house and rest for a while. It's going to be tough making it to the mine on foot." He touched her hand. "You should try to rest, as well."

She put the car in gear and eased past the deputy's parked patrol vehicle. They'd barely cleared the bumper when the deputy fired the engine and red and blue lights strobed behind them.

"You were right. He's going to stop us." Jamie breathed the words out fearfully.

Gavin watched Miller turn the vehicle around and come after them. "Relax. If he sees you're nervous, he'll suspect we're up to something."

Jamie stopped the car and drew in a shaky breath. Behind them, Miller got out of his patrol car and headed their way. Gavin prayed for strength for himself and for Jamie not to fall apart. He had a feeling that Miller was just looking for a reason to take them in.

SIX

Deputy Miller advanced with his weapon drawn. Horrified, Jamie whirled to Gavin. "He's got his gun out." She couldn't hide the terror in her voice.

Gavin clasped her hand and held it. "It's going to be okay."

She wasn't nearly as sure.

"Get out of the car with your hands up," Miller ordered when he reached the back of the car.

Jamie couldn't stop shaking. "What should we do?"

Gavin turned in his seat. "We do as he asks. Get out slowly with your hands in the air. The last thing we need is another gunshot wound to deal with."

The damage the bullet had done to Gavin's body was starting to show. He could barely get out of the car on his own. She was worried Miller would notice something off in his behavior and look closer. Would he arrest them? Or worse?

Jamie stepped out of the car and put her hands in the air. Gavin slowly did the same, his face pale, pain etched there.

"What's this about, deputy?" Gavin asked, somehow managing to keep his voice strong.

Miller motioned the gun at Jamie. "Get over there next to her."

As she watched, Gavin plastered a blank expression on his face and obliged.

"What were you two doing back there?" Miller kept the weapon trained on Gavin.

"I went to pick up a few things from my house," Jamie said. "The last time I checked that wasn't illegal. I told you where my uncle is."

Miller didn't answer. "Pop the trunk and get over there." He motioned them to the opposite side of the road.

"Dan, I'm a CIA agent. We have the right to know why you've stopped us," Gavin told him.

Miller immediately grew wary. "You joined the CIA?" He didn't seem convinced, but he changed his demeanor a little.

"That's right, and I know you're violating our civil rights by not telling us why you pulled us over…again. We told you everything we know about Paxton. Unless you have evidence that ties us to some crime, you need to proceed very carefully."

Miller actually appeared afraid. "She's related to Paxton. We believe he's guilty of murder at the very least. That gives me the right to search this vehicle if I think it's been involved in a crime."

"Only this isn't Jamie's vehicle. It's my rental car." Jamie could tell that Gavin was fading quickly.

"He's right. I'm a criminal defense attorney in Louisville. Without Gavin's permission you can't search the vehicle."

She stepped closer to Miller, hoping to keep his attention off Gavin. "And you have no proof that Uncle Paxton is guilty of anything. Even if he was, I'm certainly not responsible for his actions."

"If you aren't guilty, you won't mind me searching the car," Miller challenged. "Unless you have something to hide?"

Now was not the time to argue their civil rights. She needed to get Gavin out of here as fast as possible.

"Fine, search the car and then let us be on our way." She hoped she sounded more confident than she felt inside.

Miller popped the trunk himself, then looked around, reminding her of the way he and his partner had searched her vehicle the day before. He'd been looking for something in particular. Was that the reason he'd insisted on searching the car now?

Once Miller was satisfied there was nothing incriminating inside, he opened the driver's side back door and spotted the backpack.

"What's in here?" He shot them a questionable look, then took the bag out and unzipped it, dumping the contents onto the ground. One of the little figurines her mother used to collect broke into a dozen pieces on the pavement.

Tears filled Jamie's eyes. That was one of the few possessions that she still had of her mother's.

Miller tossed the bag on the ground beside it and headed back to his vehicle with one final warning. "You'd better be telling the truth about where Paxton is, because if I find out different, you're both in big trouble, CIA agent or not. And make sure you get that wrecked car out of the ditch as soon as possible. If we have to tow it, it'll cost you."

He got back into his vehicle and slammed the door hard. As he drove past them, he crushed the remaining pieces of the memento into dust.

Jamie hurried over to the items that were left and dropped to her knees, clutching her mother's precious collectibles against her chest.

Gavin came over, awkwardly crouching beside her. He gently put the rest of the figurines into the bag and zipped it closed. "I'm sorry about that," he murmured earnestly. "He had no right to do that."

She brushed aside tears and got to her feet, holding out her hand to him.

He took it with a grateful smile, using her strength to pull himself to his feet. He stumbled into her. Jamie put her arms around his waist to steady him, then struggled to get him back to the car.

He all but fell into the seat, and her fear for his well-being increased. Jamie quickly closed the door and grabbed the bag. Putting it on the back seat, she got behind the wheel.

Gavin leaned against the headrest with his eyes closed.

"Gavin!" She shook him, and he slowly opened his eyes.

"I'm okay." He slurred his words, indicating it was far from the truth. "We need to get out of sight as soon as possible. I don't trust Miller not to change his mind and come after us again. He can make us both disappear if he wants to."

Jamie put the car in Drive and headed down the mountain, going as fast as she dared. Once she pulled onto Ava's property, she slowed the car's speed. Every single bump in the road had Gavin cringing in pain.

"I'm sorry," she murmured, hating that she'd hurt him. She pulled the car into the garage and out of sight, hit the button to close the door and killed the engine.

Next to her, Gavin didn't move a muscle. Every time she saw him like this, she was terrified. Would he pay with his life for Miller's crimes? "Gavin, we're here."

He slowly turned his head and looked into her eyes.

"I'm going to need you to help me. I don't think I can manage it on my own."

Jamie stuffed down her fear and got out. Once she'd unlocked the home's side door, she went around to Gavin's door and opened it.

"Easy does it." She slid her arm around his waist. He flinched as he draped his arm over her shoulders and shifted sideways so that he could put his feet on the ground.

It took all of Jamie's strength to lift his tall frame out of the car. Gavin leaned heavily against her, and she struggled not to collapse beneath his weight.

They slowly moved inside the house, and she helped him over to the sofa.

"Rest now," she said once he was lying down. "Where are the pain pills?" she asked and he patted his jacket pocket.

Jamie dug them out and poured a couple of

pills into her palm, then got a glass of water from
the kitchen. She braced the back of his neck so
that he could swallow the medicine. The exertion of simply driving to her house had been too
much. How would they ever make it all the way
up Darlan Mountain to the mine?

"Gavin, what can I do to help you?" she asked,
because she was out of ideas.

He dragged in a breath and closed his eyes.
"Rest is the only thing that will help me. We'll
wait until nightfall. They'll be watching the
place, have no doubt—Miller might not be
around, but I'm guessing one of his men is.
There's no way we can give them the slip in
broad daylight. I don't think I could make it even
if we could. If we stand any chance at getting to
the mine alive, we have to wait."

Someone was shaking his arm. Frustrated, he
tried to bat the hand away. "Gavin, you have to
wake up. The sheriff is here." He recognized the
panic in Jamie's voice right away. His eyes flew
open and he stared into Jamie's frightened face.

"Is he alone?" he asked and forced his injured
body up to a sitting position.

"Yes, it's just Andy."

Gavin rubbed a hand over his sleep-weary
eyes. "We have to let him in. He knows I'm here,

at the very least. If I don't answer, he'll suspect something is up."

He stumbled to his feet with effort, unable to keep from wincing. Jamie hurried over to help steady him. Gavin closed his eyes and waited for the nausea to go away.

"I'm okay," he said once he felt a little steadier. She let him go. Gavin slowly went over to the door. Before he unlocked it, he did a quick sweep over the room, looking for any red flags. The monitor!

"Cover the screen up with a blanket," he whispered, and Jamie rushed over, grabbed the blanket from the sofa and tossed it over the monitor.

Gavin opened the door, startling Andy, who appeared ready to leave.

"I was beginning to think you weren't home, after all." Andy took a step forward.

"Sorry, Jamie and I were out back talking and I almost didn't hear you knock. Come inside." Gavin stepped away to let Lawson in.

Andy spotted Jamie and took off his Stetson politely. "Good to see you again, Jamie. I wondered where you'd gone. I stopped by your place before I came here." Andy didn't mention the carnage there and Jamie somehow managed to keep her reaction to herself.

"After what happened there last night and with

there being no electricity, well…" She left the rest unsaid.

Her comment seemed to come as a surprise to Andy. "What happened there last night?" he asked with concern.

Why hadn't Miller updated the sheriff about what they'd done?

"Your deputy and some of your men fired on us. They shot up the place, as I'm sure you're aware," Gavin told him.

Lawson turned pale. It was a moment before he could speak. "I'm sure they had reason after what happened to Terry. Terrible thing."

But Miller and his goons hadn't known about Terry until after they'd shot up the house. Gavin kept that bit of information to himself.

"Poor Terry. He was such a good man," Lawson continued. "That's actually why I'm here. You understand that I need to ask you some questions, Jamie, seeing as Terry's body was found on your property and all."

Jamie's brow knitted together in confusion. "We already told Deputy Miller that we didn't know anything about what happened to Terry."

This bit of news came as an obvious surprise to Lawson. "You did? When did you speak with Dan?"

Gavin frowned. Something was definitely off about Lawson's lack of knowledge.

"Earlier today," Gavin supplied. "He stopped us on the way back from Jamie's house. She needed to pick up a few things there. Sheriff, we don't have any idea what happened to Terry, and neither of us have seen Paxton since we got here. As Jamie told you before, he's not in town."

Lawson scanned the room. "Everything okay here?" he asked and indicated a single blood-stained bandage that had fallen off the coffee table almost out of sight. He'd missed it when he looked around the room.

Gavin's gaze locked with Jamie's. He was aware of her drawing in a shaky breath.

"Everything's fine. That must have been something Ava left out before…" He stopped short. Couldn't say the word. He still couldn't believe she was gone.

Lawson accepted his answer, but Gavin was left with the impression that he didn't really believe him.

Gavin needed to do something to take Lawson's scrutiny off the house. "Do you have a time of death for Terry?"

Lawson turned his attention back to Gavin. "The ME says sometime between six and ten last evening."

"That's a pretty wide gap. Anyone could have gone up there and killed him." Gavin knew the time of death was closer to six—around the time he'd spotted the man in the woods.

"That's true enough," Andy said and nodded. "As I recall, you and Jamie were heading up there around that time."

Jamie shifted nervously, garnering Lawson's attention again.

"We did go up there yesterday, but the power was off. Gavin offered to let me stay here."

Lawson didn't look away. "That so?"

"Yes, that's so. We left after just a few minutes. It was too dark to see anything."

There was no doubt Lawson didn't believe her. "Why didn't you get the items while you were there last night?"

Jamie let go of a breath. "Like I said, it was dark by then. There was no way I could see anything inside the house. I decided to wait until daylight. We were heading back from the house this morning when your deputy stopped us and searched us at gunpoint, which was totally unwarranted. We had done nothing wrong and were more than cooperative."

Lawson clearly had no idea what his deputy had been up to. "I'm sure he had his reasons for the search. This is a murder investigation, after all."

"What caliber of weapon was used to kill Terry?" Gavin asked, because he didn't like the direction the interrogation was going. He was positive Terry was killed with a shotgun.

The sheriff wasn't as forthcoming with this detail. "Sorry, but I can't divulge that information. This is an active investigation, and you two were in the area at the estimated time of death. You'll understand that, until I can clear you both, I can't give out details of the case."

Gavin couldn't tell if the sheriff was trying to cover up something or if he was really serious.

"I've been trying to get in touch with Paxton since yesterday. He's not answering his phone. I did some checking around Jamesville, over where the miners buy their supplies. No one remembers seeing him in the last few days. You have any idea where he really is, Jamie?" Lawson asked in a low tone that bordered on threatening.

Jamie hid her uneasiness badly. "I have no idea. He told me he was going there for supplies. Maybe he changed his mind and went somewhere else."

Lawson didn't believe it. "That's pretty strange for him to be away from the mine for so long, don't you think?"

Jamie stood up straighter and squared her shoulders. "Not really. Uncle Paxton told me that he was thinking of taking a few days off to visit some friends soon. Maybe he decided to do that instead."

Lawson finally nodded. "That makes sense. Still, if you hear from Paxton, I need to speak with him as soon as possible. Tell him to call me directly. And if you two come up with anything relevant to the investigation, I'd ask that you do the same." He donned his hat and headed for the door.

With a puzzled look Jamie's way, Gavin followed him. "Thanks for stopping by, sheriff. If we hear anything, we'll let you know."

"Where's the truck?" Lawson asked out of the blue.

At first Gavin wasn't sure what he was talking about.

"'Scuse me?"

Lawson pointed to the driveway. "Ava's truck. I didn't see it parked outside."

Gavin struggled to come up with a believable answer. "Oh…it's out back. I was cutting down some dead trees on the place."

The excuse was about as thin as the ice on William's Pond in wintertime, but it was all he could come up with.

"Speaking of, I noticed Jamie's car still up on the side of the road. I figured you hadn't had time to call your friend to tow it with everything going on. I gave him a call. He's going to pick it up sometime tomorrow."

Gavin was surprised by Lawson's kindness. "Thank you," he managed.

"No problem. It's best not to leave cars unattended for too long. You wouldn't want someone to come along and vandalize it."

He still didn't buy the sheriff's motives. "No, we would not."

Lawson looked him in the eye. "I meant what I said earlier. Let *me* know if you have anything useful."

Gavin closed the door with an uneasy feeling in the pit of his stomach. Why had Lawson been so insistent that they reach out to him and him alone? What was he up to?

SEVEN

"What was that about?" Jamie asked the second she was certain Lawson had gone.

Gavin slowly made his way back to the sofa and sank down. "It sounds as if he had no idea what Miller is up to, which is kind of strange."

She could see the effort of dealing with the sheriff had drained Gavin's energy. "You should lie down for a while and rest." She didn't want to say it aloud, but she had no idea if Gavin would be ready to make the hike up to Darlan Mountain.

Gavin shook his head. "I'm fine. I'm just trying to make sense of all of this."

She sat down next to him and took his hand. "I know you are, but it's hard. Nothing adds up. Do you think Miller is acting without Andy's permission? Andy certainly seemed in the dark about his actions."

Gavin turned so that he could look into her eyes, and her heart went crazy at the emotions she saw there. "He has a lot of other deputies working with him. How can Lawson not know?"

"Some sort of power play, you think?" she asked, and he shook his head and then leaned back against the sofa and closed his eyes. She knew no matter what was going on, he needed to rest. Otherwise, they'd never figure it out.

Jamie focused on their joined hands. "We're both tired and running on empty. Why don't you rest while I make us something to eat?"

His eyes opened and he smiled over at her. "That would be nice." When she started to get to her feet, he held her there. "I'm sorry this is happening to you, Jamie. You don't deserve any of it."

Jamie's heart went out to him. He was fighting so hard for her. She returned his smile. "You don't deserve what's happening, either. I know how hard it was for you losing your father and now Ava. I'm just so sorry, Gavin. But I'm thankful for your help. I can't imagine trying to do this alone."

His smile disappeared. He looked so serious. "You and I were friends for a long time before… well, before what happened. I'd do anything for you. Always will."

The lump in her throat made it hard to force words out. "I feel the same way about you. Maybe after this is all over, we can find our way back to being friends again." She really wanted that to happen.

Something darkened his expression. He reached up and touched her cheek gently, and her eyes closed, her heart racing in response to his touch. Was she only fooling herself, thinking they could simply be friends again?

With her emotions raw and close to the surface, she stumbled to her feet and he let her go. Without another word, she left him alone.

Jamie opened the refrigerator and stared at the meager contents without seeing them. It hurt to think about what might have been. She'd been so in love with him back then. Her world had revolved around the time they spent together. Friday night football games. Saturday night at the local drive-in in town, where all the kids went to hang out. Sunday afternoon cruising around town in Ava's old pickup truck. They'd spent every possible moment together, and yet it hadn't been enough. She'd gone to bed each night anticipating the next time she'd see him.

And then that day had happened and everything crumbled at her feet. She'd watched her father be taken away in handcuffs. Her seventeen-year-old heart couldn't take it all in. Visiting Noah at the jail with her uncle, Jamie had never seen her father look so desolate. The tears in his eyes haunted her to this day.

The trial that followed had been nothing but a sham. Her father's attorney kept insisting that he should take a plea, but Noah refused. He was innocent, and innocent people didn't go to jail.

The day the verdict came in had shattered that belief. Her father was going away for the rest of his life. There hadn't even been time to hold him one more time before he'd been escorted off to Eddyville, to the maximum security prison there.

She and Paxton had visited every chance they got. Uncle Paxton had vowed he'd find out the truth and get his brother free. It hadn't happened. Noah had died in a prison infirmary of miner's lung, and Jamie hadn't been able to get to him before he drew his final breath.

The funeral had been one of the most devastating days of her life. Jamie had thought she would never stop crying. She still remembered Ava's kindness that day, even though her father was considered a murderer by the town he once loved. Ava had organized a luncheon at the church, and she and Paxton had been treated with kindness. Jamie would forever be grateful for Ava Dalton's friendship. Now Ava was gone and someone was trying to silence Paxton for something he knew. Jamie was terrified that she and Gavin wouldn't be able to unravel the truth before it was too late and she and Paxton became the final victims of a nightmare that started ten years earlier.

Something startled Gavin awake. He looked around the darkened room. There had been movement. He'd sensed it.

Gavin struggled to a sitting position. The light from the monitor captured his attention right away. Jamie stood close by. He got to his feet and went over.

"What is it?" he asked, making her jump.

She pointed to the screen that showed the road in front of the house. "Miller came back about a half hour earlier. He was alone, until now."

There were two additional patrol vehicles out there. The reality of it sent his thoughts churning. They needed to get out.

"They're getting ready to storm the house. Jamie, whether or not they have any proof, they're going to arrest us. We have to leave now."

"There's a shortcut I remember from childhood. It should get us to my house faster. We can gather the supplies and head to the mine."

Gavin nodded. "Good. Let's get going. On foot, it's not going to be easy." He stumbled a little as he headed for the back of the place. When she didn't follow, he turned, seeing all her doubts.

"Are you sure you're up to this?" she asked.

He wasn't, but they were all out of choices. "I'll be fine." He tucked his weapon behind his back, and she grabbed the shotgun.

"I have more ammo at your place, but we need to take extra just in case Miller has people stationed at your house. I think Ava keeps some extra shotgun shells in the hall closet. I'll grab some bullets for the Glock I have in my bag along with the binoculars."

He found his backpack, shoved the medicine inside along with extra bandages, and then headed for his room when she stopped him. "I'll get them. You just take it easy."

Gavin couldn't imagine how bad he must look. He sat down at the desk and continued to watch the monitor. The men were getting out of their vehicles. They didn't have much time.

"Jamie, we've got to get out of here now," he called out, and she came running into the room. He pointed to the screen. "They're coming this way. We'll never get away in time. Not with this." He pointed to his wound.

Her troubled gaze held his.

There was only one place he could think of for them to hide out in a pinch. "Ava has that old root cellar on the place. I think I can find it in the dark. Hopefully, they won't think to check there."

He turned off the monitors and slung the backpack she'd loaded with ammo over his shoulder. "We can't afford to use a flashlight," he told her. "Stay close to me."

She followed him out the back door, and they listened carefully. "I don't hear anything." He was worried. "I don't like it."

Jamie took his hand, and together they stepped off Ava's beloved back porch and headed out. Even though the yard was well maintained, they were still walking in the dark. The clouds hid most of the stars. The moon hadn't come up yet.

"It's just over there. Getting the door open will be a pain, though," he whispered.

Once they reached the cellar a little way from the house, Gavin grabbed the door handle and pulled. It took everything inside of him to keep from screaming in pain.

"Let me help." Jamie took hold of the door with him. Together they managed to lift it. He prayed the deputies hadn't heard the noise they made, but sound carried through the hollers.

They stopped and listened. "I don't hear anything, do you?" she whispered.

"No, but let's get out of sight as quickly as possible." Gavin went inside and held out his hand to Jamie.

"Be careful, it's been years since I've been down here. I don't know what kind of shape the stairs are in."

Once she was inside, he piled as much brush as he could in front of the door and then shut it as quietly as possible. Holding hands, they slowly made their way down the steps. When he reached the bottom one, he dug out the flashlight from his backpack and shone it around. Cobwebs clung to everything in sight. The place was covered in several inches of dust. He remembered his grandmother telling him that, with her advancing years, she hadn't canned anything in a long time. The cellar had sat unused for a while.

As he flashed the light around, he quickly noticed that the condition of the place was far worse than he thought. One of the walls appeared close to collapsing. Gavin pushed aside the image of the cellar entombing them inside its dusty walls.

"We can't afford to keep the light on. With the walls in such bad shape, the flashlight's beam will show through." He turned off the light and she moved closer, shivering. He would give anything to be able to reassure her it was going to be okay, but nothing could be further from the truth. He wasn't sure how much Miller knew of the property, but most of the older houses around these parts had root cellars.

He held her tight. Being close like this reminded him of all those times in the past when he and Jamie would slip off to a quiet place to be alone. He'd hold her, as he was right now, and they'd sneak kisses. He'd been crazy about her. Back then, he'd thought he would spend the rest of his life right here in Darlan with her at his side.

He'd been wrong. Neither one of them could have foreseen the tragic outcome that would drive them apart.

Outside, the noise of footsteps could be heard, rousing him from memories of the past. The men were almost right on top of them now. Jamie clutched him tighter.

"Any sign of them?" Miller asked. He sounded as if he was just outside the door.

"No, and there's been no movement at the house. Maybe they didn't come back to the house like you thought. They could have headed out of town." A voice he didn't recognize responded.

While the conversation continued, it sounded as if they were moving away from the cellar.

"How long do you think we should wait here before we leave?" Jamie whispered.

Gavin had no idea. Miller was law enforcement. He could be standing close by, waiting for them to slip up. "A little longer. If we leave before they've cleared the area, we might be walking straight into an ambush."

EIGHT

It felt as if they'd been huddled in the rotting old root cellar for hours, and Jamie wasn't sure what the worse danger was: the men searching for them outside or the man standing a breath away.

Holding him close, she could feel Gavin's steady pulse against her ear. But her heart was breaking all over again for what might have been.

If it weren't for the danger they now faced, it might have been ten years earlier. Before Gavin's final words imprinted themselves in her head.

He moved slightly. They faced each other. Did he feel the same way?

"Jamie…" He whispered her name, his voice rough with emotion. Her breath hung in her throat at the possibilities hidden there. She couldn't go back to the hurt.

She stepped back. His hands fell away. Would there ever be a time when they could be together without the past clouding their feelings?

"How long do you think we've been here?" she asked, needing to bring things back down to a less emotional level.

He dragged in a breath. "I'm not sure. Maybe an hour." She could hear the pain in his tone. She couldn't imagine how difficult the trek through the woods had been for him.

"How are you holding up?"

"Hanging in there, I guess." He didn't sound good.

"I think I saw a chair in the corner. You should sit down for a bit."

He didn't argue. "I think that's a good idea." Gavin felt his way over to the area where the chair was and eased his weight down. Jamie heard it squeak.

He leaned back, exhausted by the effort.

Lord, he needs Your strength. Please help him, Jamie silently prayed.

Outside, a sound captured her attention. "I hear voices again," she whispered and knelt next to him.

She reached for his hand, and he held it as a flashlight's beam bounced off the holes in the walls.

"We didn't check the cellar. They could be hiding in there." A voice she didn't recognize moved closer.

"They're not in there. But just to be sure…"

Miller stopped. Before Jamie knew what the man intended, shots split the quiet of the night and whistled past them. Jamie grabbed hold of Gavin. They both hit the ground. Gavin tucked her in close, his body sheltering hers in a heroic measure that was just like Gavin.

Another round of shots kicked up dirt inches from where they lay. Then silence followed.

"Come on, let's get out of here. If they were in there, they're dead now. I don't want to have to explain this to the sheriff."

Leaves crunched beneath their feet as they walked away. After what felt like an eternity, Gavin slowly eased to his feet, holding his injured side. He dropped down to the chair. Immediately, Jamie was at his side, worried.

"Are you okay? You didn't get hit again?" Fear gripped her heart. He couldn't take much more.

Gavin barely managed an answer. "No, but I'm not okay. I think I reopened the wound."

She took the flashlight from him and shone it on his side. He was right. Blood seeped from the wound to stain his shirt.

"I put some extra bandages in the backpack," he forced out.

Jamie unzipped the bag and then helped him slide off his jacket before she unbuttoned his shirt.

"It's not too bad." It was a lie to reassure him.

Nothing could be further from the truth. The wound appeared red and inflamed. She tossed the bloodied bandage away, then packed the wound with strips of cloth and rewrapped it.

Then she knew he needed to hear the truth. "You need medical help. If this gets infected…" She didn't finish.

"I'll be okay for the moment." She wanted to believe him, but in her mind, she couldn't imagine how he was going to make it to her house, much less the mine. "Gavin, you're barely able to stand by yourself."

He framed her face and looked into her eyes, silencing her. "I'll be okay. We have to keep moving. It's our only option. Right now, they believe we've left town. That won't last for long."

His answer wasn't the one she needed, but they were all out of choices.

Jamie helped him to his feet, then grabbed the backpack and slung it over her shoulder. With the shotgun in one hand and the flashlight in the other, Gavin leaned heavily against her as they stumbled up the stairs.

"Kill the flashlight. Let me go out first," Gavin said in a near whisper. Jamie moved out of the way and let him ease the door open.

He stepped out into the dark night while Jamie's heart hammered in her ears. She couldn't hear a sound. Had Miller and his men headed back to their vehicles?

Please, God.

Gavin held out his hand. "I believe they've left," he said softly. "Let's get going. Which way to the shortcut?"

In the darkness, it was hard to find. "It's been years since I came out here. I believe it's this way." She pointed to the right, where nothing could be seen but blackness. At night, the hollers could be deadly. One wrong move and you could fall into one of the half-dozen abandoned mine shafts to your death. Or stumble off the side of the mountain.

She and Gavin started walking in the direction she'd indicated. Jamie hoped her memory proved true and they weren't running in circles.

With Gavin struggling to put one foot in front of another, Jamie tried to get her fuzzy brain to make sense of what they'd been through so far. Was this really all related to drugs? How did Sheriff Lawson fit into all of this?

"Where exactly will this way put us out at?" Gavin asked. He stopped and dragged in several labored breaths. Jamie's fear for him increased.

Somehow, she shoved aside her troubled thoughts. "Back off to the side of the house. I hope they aren't still watching it."

"Let's hope not," he managed. Guilt tore at her

heart. She'd put Gavin's life in danger by turning to him for help.

"What do you think they did with Ava's truck?" she asked.

"Probably hauled it off somewhere and searched it for whatever they were looking for at your house. They probably dumped it in one of numerous old mine shafts once they didn't find what they were looking for, to get rid of any evidence that would tie it to us. They'll do the same to you and me if they find us."

Those ominous words hung between them in the chilly night. "This has to be related to the drug problem in Darlan somehow," Gavin said, and Jamie suppressed a chill. "Still, why do they think Paxton would know anything about that?"

Jamie drew in a breath and voiced her beliefs. "Uncle Paxton told me he'd found proof that my father didn't kill yours. What if he's right and your father's death had something to do with drugs?"

Seconds ticked by before Gavin answered. "I think we should stick with what we know," he said quietly and he had no idea how much those words hurt to hear.

Jamie struggled to hold on to her composure. She didn't care what evidence they tried to falsify to prove their case against her uncle, there was no way she'd ever believe Paxton was involved in such a destructive thing.

"I can see the house." Jamie pointed up ahead, and Gavin followed her. "We're almost there." Her eyes skimmed his face, no doubt seeing the exhaustion he couldn't hide. "Do you think you can make it?" she asked gently.

He managed a nod, conserving his energy. Truth be told, he'd never been so happy to see anything than he was to see her old house. The hours in the woods had depleted what little strength he had left. It was a struggle to put one foot in front of the other.

Once they drew closer, Gavin glanced around, trying to pick up any abnormal movement. While he didn't see anything unusual, he couldn't help but feel they might be walking into an ambush. He took out his night-vision binoculars and zoomed in on the house. "I don't see anyone around the place. Let's hope it's empty."

They slowly eased down the rise and toward the back of the house.

Gavin stepped up on the porch and froze. Someone had left the back door standing slightly ajar. It hadn't been that way earlier.

"They've been here since our last visit." He pointed to the open door. "Miller must have searched the place again. Maybe he thought we left something incriminating behind."

He drew his weapon, eased the door farther open and went inside. He was almost halfway across the living room when he heard it. *Click, click, click.*

"Run, Jamie!" he yelled as he turned and ran as fast as he could, all but dragging her along with him.

They'd barely made it out the door when the house exploded. Both he and Jamie flew some twenty feet through the air.

For a moment, he lost consciousness. The heat from the fire brought him to. He stared up at the blaze. Where was Jamie?

Gavin struggled to his feet. The world around him swayed. It was as if everything had gone mute. While his hearing had taken the brunt of the explosion, he could feel blood trickling from several facial wounds.

Once the world stopped spinning, his only thought was for Jamie. Ignoring the pain in his side, he searched frantically for her. She'd landed a little way behind him. He could see her crumpled body lying still. Gavin covered the space between them as quickly as his broken body would allow, fear following him every step of the way.

"Jamie." He called out her name as he reached

her side, then knelt next to her. He felt for a pulse. After he'd assured himself it was there, he touched her arms and legs. Nothing appeared broken. She had several cuts, as well, and she was bleeding.

He shook her. "Jamie, wake up."

She slowly opened her eyes. When she saw him, she grabbed him around the waist and held him tight, shaken.

"What happened?" She barely got the words out.

"The house was set to explode when someone entered it. No doubt all entrances were wired. They were probably expecting Paxton to return."

She pulled away and stared at the blazing inferno behind him. "I can't believe it. We almost died. Gavin. What are these men after?"

He shook his head. "I wish I knew. Right now, we've got to get out of here. They'll see the explosion and come looking to see if Paxton is dead."

As if in response to his words, the sound of a vehicle could be heard making its way up the mountain toward the blaze.

"Do you think you can walk?" he asked.

She nodded. "Yes, I think so."

He wasn't nearly so sure, but they didn't have a choice. He managed to get to his feet and held out his hand. She took it and slowly stood. For a second, she leaned against him and his arms tightened around her. He wondered if she was hurt worse than he'd originally thought.

"I'm okay," she said and pulled away, the moment gone.

Behind them, the noise of a vehicle coming to a stop could be heard.

"Stay here. I'll be right back," Gavin told her, and then keeping within the coverage of the trees, he crept closer. Gavin counted at least four armed men. He slowly eased back to where Jamie was hidden. If this was Miller and his men, and they spotted them, with both of them still shaken from the explosion, Gavin wasn't so sure they would survive another run-in.

NINE

Jamie watched the men staring at the fire. She and Gavin had moved a little deeper into the woods. From where they stood, she could see the front of the house quite clearly. The men weren't there to put it out. Through the blaze, she couldn't make out who they were, but they didn't seem a bit surprised by the explosion. They were talking amongst themselves as if nothing had happened.

A cell phone rang. "No one's here," one of the men said. "We're not sure if he's inside. The fire's still burning pretty bad." The man listened for a bit. "Alright. We'll see you in a few." He ended the call. "He's on his way up here now."

Several of the men didn't appear pleased by the news. They grumbled amongst themselves, then went back to watching the fire, talking and occasionally laughing.

While Jamie and Gavin watched, another vehicle pulled up. This time Jamie recognized the deputy's SUV.

"That's Miller," she whispered.

Dan Miller got out of the vehicle and went over to the men. Jamie tried to focus on what he was saying. "I'm going down the mountain to make sure no one sees the fire and decides to come and investigate. We still don't know who set it off?"

"No, there's been no activity around. Whoever was in there is probably dead," the man who had been on the phone answered.

"Did you search around the place?" Miller demanded, clearly not satisfied with the way things had gone.

The silence that followed angered him more.

"Well, do it," Miller all but yelled at the man. "Paxton's smart and he knows we're after him."

"You heard him. Get to it." The other man took out his anger on the men with him.

"We've got to get out of here now." Gavin grabbed her hand, and they started running as fast as they could.

"Hold on. I see someone over there!" one of the men yelled. "There's two of them."

"That's Jamie and Gavin. We can't let them get out of here alive."

Her heart thundered with each step. There were five of them. Even with the weapons she and Gavin had, they couldn't hold them off long.

Gavin looked behind them. The men had cleared what was once the side of the house and were coming toward them full force. "We need a diversion."

She remembered they were close to a boarded-up mine. "There's that old abandoned mine that collapsed years ago. It's not too far from here. If we can get some space between us and those men, we can hide there."

Gavin's silence told her the idea was not a welcome one, but they were all out of options.

"Gavin, it's our only chance."

"Do you remember the location well enough to find it in the dark?"

She hadn't been there in years, but she had a general recollection of where it was.

"Yes, I can find it."

He let her hand go and she stopped, turning to face him. "What are you doing? They'll be here soon."

She saw him smile sadly. "I'm going to do an old-fashioned shoot-out. See if I can buy you some time."

Jamie shook her head. "You can't stand them off alone. You're outnumbered."

"I'll be fine. I'm right behind you. Just keep moving."

"No, Gavin." She didn't want to leave him

behind. She couldn't bear the thought of something happening to him.

"Go, Jamie." With one final look into his eyes, she turned and started running as fast as she could.

"Over there!" one of the men yelled and started firing in Jamie's direction. She barely made it behind a tree before bullets rushed past her.

When there was silence again, she started running and didn't look back.

Behind her, more shots fired, followed by another weapon engaging. Gavin.

Someone yelped in pain. It took everything inside of her not to turn around and go back to make sure he was okay. She knew she couldn't do that. Gavin was a trained CIA agent. Better equipped to handle the situation than she was, even wounded.

Jamie reached the area where the abandoned mine had collapsed. It had once been one of the oldest working mines in Darlan County. In the dark, and trying to recall the location from memory, it took longer than she'd expected, but she finally found the boarded-up hole in the side of the mountain. Nothing about it was inviting.

The mine had been sealed off for a long time, since she was a child. When it had collapsed, it had trapped six miners below. The rescue team hadn't made it to the site of the disaster in time to save any of them.

Jamie yanked away enough boards to get inside. Shoving aside her fear of spiders and creepy-crawly things, she squeezed through the opening and did her best to replace the boards in case the men happened her way.

What if the area where she stood was unstable? It had been years since anyone had been in here. If it collapsed, she'd be buried alive. With difficulty, she shoved the fear aside. She was trying to save her uncle's life. She had to be strong.

The gunfire had stopped. Where was Gavin? She couldn't let herself consider that he might have been captured, or worse.

As Jamie stared into the blackness surrounding her, she heard something alarming nearby— what sounded like footsteps coming her way at a fast pace.

She clasped her hand over her mouth as the steps halted next to the mine. Someone shoved one of the boards free. Jamie inched away from the entrance as a flashlight's beam illuminated the area where she had just been.

"I don't see anyone. The place is unstable. They wouldn't hide there. Let's keep going."

After a moment, the footsteps faded into the distance. Jamie let go of the breath she'd held on to.

Just as she'd begun to relax, another set of footsteps came to a stop next to the mine entrance.

"Jamie, are you in there?" Gavin whispered so quietly that she almost didn't hear him. Relief overtook her fear.

"Yes, I'm in here." She thanked God for keeping him safe.

He shoved the rest of the boards free and held out his hand to her. She ignored it, going straight into his arms and holding him tight. Happy to be out of the musty mine.

"Which way were they heading?" he asked when she finally let him go.

She pointed up ahead. "Toward the Darlan Mountain Mine. Gavin, what if Uncle Paxton's in there somewhere hurt?"

With Gavin close by, they started walking toward the mine at a fast pace while Jamie tried to control her fears.

She didn't want to think what would happen to her uncle if those men stumbled on him in the belly of the mine.

"We need to reach the mine before they do." Gavin couldn't believe what had just taken place. In the firefight, he'd managed to hit one of the men. Soon after, he'd heard a vehicle leaving. He assumed it was Miller going down the mountain to make sure no one else happened their way. Miller was a coward who didn't care if his men got injured trying to protect whatever illegal activity he and the rest of his team were up to.

To stand a chance of saving Paxton, they'd have to reach the mine before the men.

He and Jamie had been walking for a little while when he heard a noise behind them that sounded like more vehicles coming up the mountain and he turned. Two patrol vehicles, with their lights flashing, rolled up on the scene of the fire. No one got out. Was Andy Lawson in one of them? Gavin had no idea how Andy fit into the picture. He hadn't been part of the previous attack at the house, and he hadn't been lying in wait outside Ava's home. Was he the person calling the shots?

"You think they'll call the fire department to put the fire out, or will they let it burn to the ground?" Jamie asked with emotion weighing in her voice. This was her family home. She'd lived there most of her life.

Gavin tugged her into his arms. "They were hoping they killed the person they were after, namely Paxton, but now they know it was us inside the house. They won't let up. They'll let the fire burn itself out, and then they'll cover the whole thing up, somehow."

"They have to be stopped. We can't let them

get away with this." He could tell she was close to losing it.

He turned her in his arms so that he could look into her eyes. "They won't. I promise you, I'm not going to let them get away with what they've done."

She held him close and nodded against his chest. He'd do everything in his power to figure out what was happening here.

"One thing is for sure. If they set the explosives to catch Paxton, then he's still alive and out there somewhere. And the sooner we get to him, the better." He just hoped they located Paxton before the men looking for him.

"You're right. We have to find him before they do."

The cloudy night made the going more difficult the higher up the mountain they went. Still, Gavin didn't dare risk using the flashlight to light their way. It would be a glaring beacon to those men.

"What I can't understand is why Paxton hasn't been living at the house. How long have Miller and his men been chasing him?" Gavin wondered aloud.

"I can't believe I had no idea what was happening to him. Every time I spoke with him, he never let on that anything was wrong. I just assumed he was staying at the house still." She sighed softly. "I noticed he'd cleared a lot of space behind the place. He told me a while back that he wanted to do some farming back there. It doesn't make sense."

She was right. Why had Paxton cleared the area only to let the power be shut off? "You can't think of anything he might have said in passing that might help us clear up what's really happening here?"

He had to believe that Paxton would have mentioned something about the situation to his niece, if only by accident.

She thought about it for a second. "When he called this last time, he mentioned that he didn't trust any police, especially the sheriff's office here, and hadn't for a while. When I asked him why, he never could tell me anything in particular. Or maybe he was afraid to say it over the phone." She looked up at him. "I'm sorry. I should have pressed him for answers. I just thought…well, I thought he was being Uncle Paxton." She stopped for a second. "He loved my father so much, and he was determined not to let him take the blame for killing yours."

Gavin didn't want to have this discussion again. He admired her loyalty to her father, but he couldn't share her faith in Noah's innocence.

One of Gavin's previous conversations with Ava ran through his head. She'd defended Noah fervently as well, refusing to believe him guilty. Ava, Noah and Paxton had always been close, along with his father.

When he couldn't think of anything to say, they continued walking again.

"What do you think Miller and his men are really up to by escalating the violence?" Jamie asked when the silence between them grew.

There was only one answer that made sense in Gavin's mind. "They're trying to cover up something. Probably something they're involved in that Paxton found out."

Jamie shook her head. "Like what?"

"I'm not sure. Ava seemed particularly worried about the influx of drugs into the area causing an increase in crime. She blamed the sheriff's office for not doing more to curtail the drugs."

"I remember her telling me the same thing," Jamie said, making him curious as to how often she'd spoken to his grandmother.

"She always was crazy about you. I'm glad you two stayed in touch."

Jamie smiled at him. "We didn't talk as often as we should have. That was my fault. There were certain things that we just couldn't move beyond and it was hard…" She stopped, but he understood.

"Still, thank you for keeping in touch with her. I admit, there were times when it was hard for me to talk to her as well. Too many bad memories, I guess."

He didn't say as much, but calling Ava had been difficult because every time he spoke to her it reminded him of the woman he'd lost.

It was the main reason he'd left Darlan behind in the first place. Everywhere he looked, he'd seen the past. His father. Jamie. What might have been. Yet the guilt was still there, even after he left and Ava had needed him. Oh, she would never have said as much, but she'd wanted her only family member close. Instead, he'd been running from a troubled past he couldn't escape, and it had tainted his entire existence.

He couldn't imagine where his life might have gone if he hadn't joined the Scorpions. After his marriage ended, he'd been in a bad place. Several times, he'd called Ava, wishing he could pour out his darkest thoughts to her, but he hadn't been able to say a word. He hadn't even told his grandmother that he'd gotten married in the first place. How was he going to tell her he'd made a mess of it? Through his brothers and sisters in the Scorpion unit, he'd found God and his life had been changed.

Still, he regretted the way things ended between himself and Emily. She was sweet and kind and she reminded him of Jamie. He'd been drawn to her because of the bad place he'd been in since his father's murder. They'd met while he was back in the states in between missions. He'd been searching for something positive and latched onto her light. They'd eloped after knowing each other less than a month and it wasn't long before the marriage started to fracture.

Emily wanted to meet his grandmother, but Gavin always had one excuse or another not to. Mostly, he believed he knew Ava would tell him he'd acted irrationally. She'd have been right. He had been floundering and grabbed on to Emily hoping she could save him.

His drive to succeed became another way of dealing with his grief. And if he was being truthful, Gavin had realized his marriage was a mistake as well. He'd thrown himself into his work more because of it, leaving Emily alone for long periods of time. Soon, it became too much for her to bear and she filed for divorce. He'd failed her.

Gavin would give anything to be able to go back in time and rewrite the past. Apologize to

Emily. Be there for his grandmother. Believe Jamie. But he couldn't, and he had to live with the results of his decisions for the rest of his life.

TEN

They reached the rise above the Darlan Mountain Mine. Down below, the trailer that had served as an office for as long as Jamie could remember appeared dark. Nothing stirred.

Jamie started down toward it, but Gavin stopped her. "Hang on a second. We need to make sure it's clear." He unzipped his backpack and took out the binoculars once more, then scanned the building and the surrounding area. "I see them." He knelt down low and Jamie followed.

"Where are they?" she asked.

He pointed to the edge of the woods close by. "Over there. They're heading for the trailer." He handed her the binoculars. Three men advanced on the trailer. While two waited outside, the third went in. In a matter of seconds, the man returned to his friends.

Jamie listened carefully as their voices carried from the valley below. "No one's been here since the last time we searched the place," one of the men said, then murmured something Jamie couldn't catch.

"We'd better check the mine. They might be hiding in there," another man said.

The third man, who had been talking on his phone, went back over to where his buddies were. "Hold up a second. He wants us back at the house. Something's come up."

One of the men wasn't happy with the new orders. "They could be in there. We can take care of the problem once and for all."

"And I told you he wants us back at the house now. Something's going on," phone man barked, not liking that his orders were questioned.

The second reluctantly turned away. "Alright, but if they get away because we missed them inside, it's on him."

The three slowly eased back into the woods and out of sight.

Jamie let out a breath, then looked at Gavin. "What do you think that was about?"

The worried expression on his face didn't ease Jamie's mind any. "I have no idea, but I sure hope they haven't found Paxton."

If she and Gavin were wrong and Paxton wasn't in the mine, then it might cost her uncle his life.

"My gut tells me he's in the mine somewhere.

This might be our only chance to check it out without them watching it," Gavin told her. "First, let's take a look inside the trailer."

As they drew near, Jamie could see broken glass everywhere. The place had been broken into by Miller's men. With her weapon at the ready, Jamie prepared herself to enter, with no idea what they'd find inside.

"Wait, Jamie." Gavin stopped her before she could go inside. She turned to him. "Let me check it out first." He was afraid of what they'd find inside.

As they stood facing each other, inches apart, Gavin unexpectedly touched her face. The tenderness in his eyes sent her heartbeat racing.

"I'll be right back." He dropped his hand and turned away, and she gathered in a much-needed breath.

Within seconds of entering the trailer, Gavin came back out. "You need to see this."

Jamie followed him. She stopped just inside the door and stared in disbelief at what she saw there. The file cabinet was open and files had been scattered all around. Paxton's desk was turned over.

"Oh, no." She clasped her hand over her mouth at what she saw on Paxton's office chair—what looked like more bloodstains in several spots. Coupled with what they'd found at her house,

Jamie was almost certain something terrible had happened to Uncle Paxton.

Gavin spotted the blood, too, and came to her side. "We don't know that it's Paxton's."

She managed a nod. "What were they searching for in here?"

He looked around at the chaos and shook his head. "I don't know."

She scanned the interior of the trailer. Half of the file folders were empty of paperwork.

"What was in the files?" Gavin asked, evidently noticing the same thing.

Jamie shook her head. "In the past, it was just purchase orders for supplies and such and employee information, but as far as I know, the mine hasn't been working in months. Besides Terry, there are no other employees."

"Why would they care about a few purchase orders or employee records?" Gavin asked.

She shook her head. "What happened to make them leave like that before they searched the mine?" Had they found Uncle Paxton?

Gavin pulled her closer. "It could be anything. The sooner we get inside the mine, the sooner we have answers."

While he was right, she dreaded going down in there again. The last time stood out in her mind. She'd come here after they'd found her father standing next to Charles's lifeless body.

She'd stared at the bloodstained ground and couldn't believe what was happening.

"Are you okay?" Gavin asked. The concern in his eyes told her he'd read her thoughts.

She managed a nod and he let her go. Jamie watched him kneel down and pick up several of the files lying on the floor.

"This one's marked revenue." He grabbed another one. "Purchase orders." Several papers were in the file. "There's certainly nothing of any importance here. Why take the files…unless…"

"They were looking for something else. Maybe they thought they'd find a clue as to where whatever they're missing might be found. Maybe that's why they took some of the file contents," Jamie reasoned.

"I don't think Paxton would take the chance of leaving anything important here, where he knew they could gain access easily enough." Gavin said, unconvinced.

Jamie lifted her shoulders. "You're right, it sounds silly. Knowing Uncle Paxton the way I do, I can't see it, either."

Gavin got to his feet and tossed the file folders down on the floor once more. "We're not going to get any answers here. Let's get to the mine."

They left the trailer, and Gavin flipped on his flashlight. "Hopefully, those men are far enough away that they won't see the light. We're going to need it down there."

She sensed his reluctance to enter the mine, and she certainly understood. He'd come to the mine and seen his father lying dead. Going back down there would bring back the ugly memories of that day.

As they headed to the gaping black void that was the entrance, Jamie couldn't help but feel as if the truth behind the decade-old murder that had been hidden for so long was about to rise, finally, to the surface. One way or another.

Gavin hadn't been inside the mine since they'd found his father. After what happened to Charles, he'd sworn never to go down there again. Yet here he was. He had to put aside the devastating memories of that day, and help Jamie find Paxton.

Still, it was hard to push aside all that he'd lost. He stopped at the entrance, stuck in place. Unable to put one foot in front of the other.

Jamie turned back to him. "I know it's hard," she said gently.

He managed a smile. "It is. I haven't been here since…that day."

She took his hand. "Me, either. You can do this, Gavin. I know you can."

The fear in her eyes urged him on. She needed him. He'd do it for Jamie.

He squeezed her hand and then aimed the flashlight through the entrance. Drawing in deep breaths, together they went inside to purge old memories once and for all.

The temperature dropped by degrees the farther down they went. The place was just as dark and dank as he remembered.

Right away, it became clear it hadn't been a working coal mine in quite some time. The road used to access the mine was showing signs of lack of use. There were more pot holes than road left, which seemed to indicate the mine hadn't been in use much longer than what Paxton had indicated to Jamie. So, what had her uncle been doing down here, if not mining, and why did Terry have to lose his life?

The ceiling was so low that they had to bend over to walk. They reached the spot where the single mine shaft divided into two separate tunnels.

"Which way?" Gavin asked. The one to the right was where they'd found his father. He didn't want to go that way.

Gavin couldn't hide his unease from her. "There's nothing much going on to the left. That's just where the supplies are stored, if I remember correctly."

He drew in a breath. "Okay, right it is."

Gavin flashed the light down the tunnel. The narrow entrance did little to reassure him.

They started walking, their steps echoing off the walls. Maintaining a bent-over position was hard on the back. Gavin could feel the stress on his injured side, too. As hard as he tried, he couldn't shake the bad feeling growing in the pit of his stomach. What if they were walking into a trap? He didn't understand why the men had suddenly backed away from hunting them. They knew he and Jamie were still out here. The mine was the only logical place for them to go. So why let them get away?

They reached another fork. A similarly narrow shaft veered off to the right and looked as if it was ready to collapse. He didn't like the looks of it.

Jamie shook her head. "This part of the tunnel wasn't there the last time I was here."

"You're right, but I feel we have to check it out." He flashed the light down the passageway. It seemed to go on for a long way.

As they made their way farther into the bowels of the mountain, the shaft suddenly ended. Gavin examined the wall closely, then tapped it with the flashlight. "It's fake," he exclaimed in disbelief.

Jamie came up beside him. "Why would my

uncle build a fake wall?" Their eyes met as they both realized. Something valuable was hidden behind it.

"Let's find out." Gavin slammed the end of the flashlight against the wall, and pieces easily crumbled away. In no time, he'd made a hole large enough to crawl through.

Behind it, they found something alarming.

"Oh, no." Jamie stared in shock. "Gavin, is that…"

"Yes, heroin, and lots of it." Gavin couldn't believe what he was seeing. Had Ava been right all along and everything that had happened to them so far, his father's death, even, came down to a bunch of drugs? If so, how did Paxton fit into what they'd uncovered?

Jamie went over to the stacks of drugs. "But why is it here?" she wondered aloud.

Gavin didn't want to voice the obvious, but she must have seen the look on his face.

"No way. No matter how bad it looks, Uncle Paxton's not involved in these drugs."

He wanted to believe her, but someone had obviously brought the drugs in and gone to great lengths to keep them hidden. Paxton was the obvious choice.

Gavin didn't voice his thought aloud. "Whatever is really going on here, we need help now, because this thing has gotten way out of hand."

He knew getting anyone from law enforcement involved wasn't something she wanted to do, but in his opinion, they were all out of choices.

Before she could answer, a noise echoed through the mine.

"What was that?" Jamie asked.

Gavin turned. He could hear voices coming from behind them. "Miller's men. They're coming after us. We have to hurry."

He grabbed her hand, and still in a doubled-over position, they made their way back to the main tunnel. Once they were back on track, they raced down the narrow passage and deeper into the mine.

"I see them up ahead." Miller! He and his men were closing in.

"The drugs are here as well," one of Miller's men yelled.

"Leave the heroin where it is for now. Hurry up. They're getting away," Miller ordered.

Shots rang out behind them, bouncing off the walls and dislodging rocks.

Was Miller crazy or just that desperate? One false shot and the whole place could come down. "Hurry, Jamie. This place is unsteady. It could collapse at any moment." As they continued running down the narrow passage, Gavin pulled Jamie in front of him. "Keep going," he told her when she turned back to him, confused.

He wasn't going to let one of those stray bullets strike her. He'd die first.

They moved as fast as they could. Up ahead, the passage suddenly split into two separate directions.

"Which way?" Jamie said in a tense whisper.

Gavin had no idea. "Just pick one." Before they could choose a passage, the world around them rumbled and shook.

"Get down!" Gavin grabbed Jamie and ducked as low as he could as huge chunks of rock splintered from the crumbling walls inches from them. The mine was caving in around them. Close by, the ceiling rained to the floor beneath the compromised walls, and immediately the world was plunged into darkness as dust and debris became so thick that he could taste it.

The flashlight fell from his hand. Gavin could feel the grit from the blanket of dust covering both him and Jamie, instantly filling his lungs. He coughed violently and wiped tears from his eyes. Jamie buried her face against his chest. It felt as if the world would never be steady again. And then an eerie silence replaced the noise.

Gavin tried to collect his thoughts. They were trapped inside the mine with their outside air supply cut off and surrounded by dense black. And Miller and his men now had access to the drugs. They didn't need Gavin and Jamie any longer. They'd let them die down here, and no one would ever be the wiser.

Jamie coughed and tried to clear her lungs of the dust while Gavin searched around for the flashlight and found it. He tried the switch. Nothing. The flashlight had broken in the collapse.

Near the place where the tunnel had caved in, Gavin heard footsteps. Someone was coming close.

"Let's get out of here," Miller said. "There's no way they're getting out alive. Come on, we need to move the drugs to a safe place."

Footsteps faded. Miller and his men had entombed them down here. Would it prove to be their final resting place?

ELEVEN

The pitch blackness surrounding them was terrifying. The air was clogged with coal dust. Jamie fought back fear. She didn't want to die here without knowing what had happened to her uncle. With no idea where the two shafts would lead, they had to keep moving. Keep fighting. "Gavin, we can't let them win. We can't die down here."

In the darkness, he gently framed her face. He was so close, and she needed him so much. "I'm not going to let that happen. We are not going to die down here. We'll locate Paxton and find out what's really going on with the drugs," he assured her with so much confidence that she almost believed him.

Gavin got to his feet and pulled her up beside him. For a moment, she clung to his strength.

"I'm right here. I'll always be right here," he said and held her close.

"I'm so glad you are. I can't imagine going through this without you."

His lips brushed across her forehead. "I'm glad I'm here, too." He took out his phone and flipped on the flashlight app, illuminating the rubble surrounding them.

Jamie looked around at the destruction. "If we'd been standing closer to the collapsed side, we might both be dead."

"Don't think about that now," Gavin told her. Even covered in dust, he'd never looked more handsome.

She managed a smile for his sake. "We both look like we've survived a war."

He chuckled at her description. "Yeah, but we're alive, and that's all that matters. Let's keep moving. We need to find another way out of here and fast." She knew he didn't want to say it, but their air supply would only last so long.

"I'm not sure which path to take."

Gavin shone the light both ways. "I don't think these passages were here the last time we were in the mine. Your uncle added them for a reason. Maybe he was expecting something like this to happen, and he wanted to be prepared for it."

Jamie prayed that in the process of digging out the extra passages, Uncle Paxton had found another way out of the mine.

"Let's go right," Jamie said and he nodded. It

was as good a choice as any. While they came prepared to go into the mine, their resources would sustain them for only so long.

They headed down the passage with no idea where the path would lead them. What if they ran into another dead end? They'd be trapped inside their own tomb.

Her mind kept going back to the heroin they'd found and what Miller had said about it. "Do you think the sheriff's department is involved in smuggling drugs?" Until recently, the thought would have been unimaginable.

"It's looking more like they are. What I don't understand is why."

Was it just her imagination, or was it getting harder to breathe? "I can't help but believe, we're missing something important that will tie everything together."

Gavin shook his head, helpless. "I've been racking my brain trying to come up with something that would shed some light on the situation. There has to be more going on here than Miller and his men smuggling drugs. Something bigger…" He stopped, his gaze latching onto hers. "I remember something my grandmother told me shortly after my father died. She mentioned that a corporation had started buying up lots of the old mines across Kentucky. They approached my dad about buying the Darlan Mountain Mine.

My dad had refused their offer flat out. Ava said Dad mentioned that he felt threatened by the man who came to see him." Gavin shook his head, frustrated. "I'm not sure what that has to do with anything, though."

She thought about what he'd said. "Maybe nothing, but it's certainly curious and the same thing happened to Uncle Paxton not too long ago. He said some people offered to buy the mine from Ava. She still had controlling rights, but she'd turned over the management of the mine to Paxton. When he told Ava about the offer, she refused to sell out right." Jamie stopped walking and faced him. "Did Ava tell Sheriff Lawson about the threat at the time? It certainly would indicate someone else might have had a reason to harm your father."

Gavin shook his head. "She tried. But the sheriff wouldn't listen. He felt he had enough evidence to convict Noah for killing Charles. The case was closed."

Jamie couldn't believe she'd never heard the story from Ava. "As far as I know, she never mentioned the previous offer to Uncle Paxton. Still, it's strange. Do you think it was the same person who offered to buy the mine before?" She hesitated. "Gavin, maybe the people trying to buy the mine are the ones who really killed your father."

The disbelief in his eyes hurt like crazy. He still believed Noah was capable of killing his father. Nothing had changed.

"As much as I want to believe you, Noah was convicted of the murder and there was never any evidence to prove someone else was involved," he said quietly. His answer was not what she wanted to hear and she struggled to keep it together. "I'm sorry, but I'm not ready to go there yet."

What little hope she held on to evaporated. Would he ever believe her? She lifted her chin. "You may not be, but there's no doubt in my mind my father didn't kill yours." Yet arguing this point again wasn't getting them anywhere and they were running out of time.

Jamie drew in a steadying breath, then let the resentment go. "There's plenty of abandoned mines around. Why not use them instead of calling attention to themselves by trying to buy out the Darlan Mountain Mine?" She shook her head. "And how do these people fit in the heroin trade, if at all? What does any of this have to do with the sheriff's office?" she said in a frustrated tone.

"For one, most of the abandoned mines around have collapsed. They'd have to dig them out to store anything there. Still, it would make more sense than buying an active mine and shutting it down. Something's off here, I just don't know what." He shrugged helplessly. "Maybe I'm being naïve, but I can't help but believe that Andy Lawson isn't involved in this thing."

Jamie couldn't share his belief. "How can he not be? He's the sheriff. Those are his men."

Gavin stood his ground. "I know, but I remember Andy from school. He was a punk and he got himself into a lot of trouble growing up, but I don't think he's capable of murder."

While she didn't share his opinion of Andy's innocence, Gavin was a trained officer. He'd faced this kind of thing more times than she had. "You think Dan Miller is the mastermind behind it all?" Jamie knew the man somewhat from the past. He was intelligent, but she didn't believe he would have come up with the plan to smuggle drugs through the county on his own.

"It's possible, I guess. Miller is certainly cunning enough, but I think this is beyond his scope. There's a bigger player involved here."

Jamie couldn't imagine who that might be. Right now, however, she was just terrified they would run out of air before they could get out of the mine alive.

Gavin tried the phone. "There's no service. I'm not surprised. We're pretty far under the mountain, but we're heading north."

"That means we're heading in the direction

of the wilderness. Gavin, there are miles and miles of woods out there. If we make it out of here alive, we'll have to hike out."

Remaining positive was a hard thing to do under their circumstances. If they found a way out, trying to navigate their way through the wilderness surrounding the mine could prove its own challenge, not to mention the unpredictable weather. It was just the two of them with limited resources and no one looking for them. They were in big trouble.

With every breath they took sucking up what precious little air remained in the mine, Gavin's faith was faltering, but he wasn't about to give in to the doubts. He had to keep fighting.

Being with Jamie again made him realize that he'd never stopped caring for her. The argument she'd made concerning the people trying to buy the mine being connected to his father's death made sense, but why hadn't any of this come out before now if it were true? Still, whatever the truth proved to be, whether his father's murder was at the hands of Noah or someone else, together they'd figure it out, then maybe they could finally break the shackles of the past.

Yet as hard as he tried, he couldn't understand how the heroin and the sheriff's department might be connected to the big business trying to buy his family's mine. Without more to go on, it was useless to speculate. Survival was the only thing that mattered now, and he needed something to take his mind off their impossible situation. He found himself wondering about Jamie's life back in Louisville.

She had grown into a strong woman in spite of what she'd had to overcome. She'd weathered the storms thrown at her, and she was still standing.

"Tell me about your life now. Are you happy?" he asked, because he wanted her to be.

She didn't look at him. He sensed it wasn't a subject she liked to talk about. Especially with him.

"I suppose. As happy as anyone can be with the past we have. I love my job. Helping others who are wrongfully accused get their freedom back feels like I'm helping my dad a little." She shrugged.

He stopped and reached for her hand. "I'm sorry you had to go through that."

She turned to face him, swallowing hard. She looked into his eyes and his heart broke. The pain he saw there assured him how difficult her father's conviction and death had been for her to deal with. He should have been there for her.

Gavin drew her close, wishing for a second chance with her. Their eyes held and he brushed a strand of hair from her face. Even covered in dust, her hair powdered white, she was beautiful, and her beauty stirred him inside.

"Regardless of what happened between my father and yours, you needed me and I let you down." He tipped her chin. Saw tears in her eyes. Hated himself for his part in her pain. He leaned close. Her eyes closed, and his lips claimed hers. The tiniest of sobs escaped before she kissed him back with all the pent-up emotions from their past. The danger they faced, the death that was closing in all around them, just faded away. It was the two of them again and it felt like she belonged in his arms.

Jamie pushed free suddenly, and he let her go. She turned away. The past and its heartache was still standing between them. Would it always be?

More than anything, Gavin wished he could believe what she said about Noah's innocence. Yet the conviction wouldn't let him.

"We should keep going. There has to be another way out. We just have to find it."

Gavin let the past go and glanced around, spotting something he hadn't seen before. A small light off to the right. As much as he wanted to believe it was a way out, he knew it wasn't. It would still be dark out. Still, it was something they needed to investigate.

"Look over there." He pointed to the light. "What is that?"

He and Jamie went closer. "It's a door." He tried to open it. "It's not budging." Their gazes locked.

"Uncle Paxton," Jamie said. "He must be in there."

"Can you hand me your shotgun?" he asked, and she gave it to him. He slammed the butt of the weapon hard against the door. It took several tries before it flew open and they faced a room filled with light.

"Let's go see what's inside," he told her and went through the door first. What he saw was shocking. There were several file cabinets set up, much like those in the trailer.

He went over to the first one and pulled out a file, letting out a low whistle at what he saw there. "Paxton clearly hasn't been mining for a while, but he has been gathering massive amounts of evidence." Jamie looked over his shoulder. "There are dozens of files with surveillance photos in here. Look at this one." He pointed to it.

It was at an abandoned building she didn't recognize. It had been taken at night and was grainy, but she spotted Dan Miller and one of the other deputies talking to a well-dressed man.

"Who do you think that is?" she asked.

"I have no idea. What's he up to with these guys?" Gavin pulled out another file, and what he saw inside was alarming. "We've got a bigger problem than we thought. Look at this." He showed her some notes written by Paxton. "Jamie, I recognize this name, Jacob Ericson. He's the head of the Southern Mafia."

She stared up at him as if trying to comprehend the significance. "Why would the Southern Mafia be involved in this unless…it's their drugs. The deputies are moving their drugs for them."

Gavin had come to the same conclusion. "That'd be my guess, too. Looks like the Southern Mafia has bought out the local law enforcement."

He dug another file out. "Paxton sure did his homework. He has a picture of our mystery man with Ericson. I wonder what he has to do with the Southern Mafia."

Jamie grabbed a separate file and scanned it. "I don't know. What do you know about the Southern Mafia?"

While he and his team had been working a weapons smuggling case recently, the FBI had shared some intel with them. The Sothern Mafia was one of the biggest drug organization in the South.

He told her what he'd learned. "They have a stronghold in just about every Southern state, and Ericson rules the entire operation with an iron fist. You don't screw over this guy and live."

Gavin recalled something he'd heard recently about an attempt on Ericson's life that had almost worked. He told her about it. "Ericson was almost killed in a bombing. Someone rigged his car to explode when he opened the door."

His gaze locked with hers. "Just like the explosives used on your house. If you ask me, someone is trying to take over Jacob Ericson's empire, and they don't care who they kill in the process. My guess is, it's the man in the photo."

Gavin could almost read Jamie's thoughts, yet in his mind, all the information they'd uncovered so far made him even more justified in believing that what they were dealing with now had nothing to do with Charles's death.

TWELVE

"You think our mystery man is trying to take over control of the Southern Mafia?" Jamie asked in disbelief.

"That would be my guess."

Jamie pulled out another file marked Mines Purchased Recently. "Oh, no. Here's a list of all the mines that have been bought over the past few years." She recognized Paxton's handwriting next to each entry.

"Look at this." She pointed to the letter written next to each of them. "What do you think he means by I?"

Gavin stared at it for a second. "Inactive. I'm guessing these inactive mines are no longer being dug for coal. I can understand why they'd want to buy up the inactive mines. If it's private property, no one should come snooping around asking questions, but why would they want to buy the Darlan Mountain Mine? It's still semi-active. What are these guys up to?"

Jamie looked at him without answers. "Whatever it is, we have to stop them."

"The question is how? And how did our mystery guy, or the Southern Mafia, get the deputies and maybe even the sheriff to work for them? Are they all corrupt?"

In Jamie's mind, it certainly appeared so. "Maybe they're helping this guy move the drugs from mine to mine." It made sense in a way. Who better to move heroin than the people who were supposed to be keeping the county safe?

Yet none of the evidence Paxton had gathered cleared Noah's name. If she and Gavin died down here, they might never know.

With each breath, Jamie could feel their oxygen supply evaporating. "Gavin, we're running out of air," she said in alarm.

Desperate, he looked around for some way out, but the room appeared to be carved into the mountain.

He tried his cell phone. "Still nothing," he said without hope.

Whoever was behind this was willing to go to deadly extremes to keep his past deeds buried forever.

"Let's go back out to the passage and see where it takes us," Jamie said. She was trying to put on a brave front, but in truth, she was scared to death of dying in the mine.

Gavin squeezed her hand, and they left the storage room and continued down the narrow shaft.

"How do you think Paxton managed to build these tunnels by himself?" she asked, because she had to think of something to take her mind off their critical situation.

Gavin looked around. "It must have taken him years."

"If Paxton did all this, then he had to have created another way out," she said.

He looked down at her and smiled. "It makes sense to me."

She could see exhaustion in his eyes. His injury was slowing him down, making it hard to put one foot in front of the other.

"How are you holding up?" she asked. She was worried about him. His expression drawn.

"I'm okay," he managed, but she didn't believe him. He couldn't go on much longer.

They'd walked about a quarter of a mile farther when Jamie noticed something unusual about the stone wall to her right. The coloring didn't match the rest of the wall. She knocked on it. It sounded hollow.

Gavin halted next to her. "What is it?"

"I think this is another fake wall."

Gavin tapped the wall. "You're right. It's not made of rock at all. It feels thin, like sheetrock."

"Can we break through it?"

"I'm pretty sure." He smashed the butt of his weapon against the wall. Chunks of sheetrock splintered from the site. Jamie took the shotgun and did the same. As they worked, more and more pieces fell free until there was a gaping hole in it. Nothing but darkness appeared before them.

Jamie continued to chip away at the hole until it was big enough to climb through.

"Let me go first," Gavin insisted. She wasn't surprised by his concern. He was always good at looking out for her.

"Be careful. We don't know what's on the other side." He looked deep in her eyes. There was so much more that she wanted to say, but now was not the time.

Gavin stepped through the hole and flashed the light around. "Oh, no…" But he didn't finish. Something crashed to the ground, and then the room grew dark once more.

"Gavin!" she screamed and didn't hesitate before scrambling through the hole to help him. She couldn't let anything happen to Gavin. "Gavin, are you okay?" Jamie had barely cleared the entrance when she slammed into Gavin. He'd stopped inches from the opening.

"What is it?" She had just gotten the words out when she realized why he'd stopped so suddenly. The sound of a shotgun being racked sent fear through her. They'd come this far only to die here in this dark hole without any answers.

"Don't hurt her," she heard Gavin say. "She's not part of this."

Nothing but silence followed. Jamie's hands shook. The pitch dark was broken by a light so piercing that it was blinding. Her nerves frayed.

Jamie tried a last-ditch effort to save their lives. "Please, we're trying to find my uncle. He mines this place and he's missing. We're trying to help him because we think he may be hurt."

The light in her eyes moved, and she could see again. She prayed this man wasn't connected to the deputies.

"Jamie? Is that you?" Jamie barely recognized her uncle's voice. He sounded so weak.

"Paxton!" The light dropped to the ground near the man. She realized it was the type of flashlight that miners used to mount to their safety helmets. Paxton had taken his off.

Jamie hurried to her uncle's side. Laying the shotgun down, she couldn't believe he was right there with them. It was then that she noticed the pain marring his kindly face.

"You're hurt," she exclaimed when she saw the way his right leg was stretched out in front of him. "You've been shot."

He collapsed onto the ground, perspiration

beading his forehead. "Yes, but I'll be okay. I'm not letting a couple of thugs take me down."

"I can't believe it." Jamie pulled him close again. He was alive. Thanks be to God, her uncle was still alive.

Gavin dropped down next to Jamie. "Have you been down here all along?" he asked the man in amazement.

Paxton managed a tiny nod.

Gavin took Paxton's light and shone it on the man's injured leg. It looked as if it hadn't been attended to at all. "What happened to you?"

"That deputy shot me in the leg!" Paxton exclaimed and then leaned back and closed his eyes. The very act of speaking took its toll.

Jamie shot Gavin a look. "When was this? Was it Dan Miller who shot you?"

Paxton shook his head. "No, one of the other deputies, but I think he was acting on Miller's orders. It happened the day I called you." Paxton peered up at her. "I went up to the house. I knew it was too soon for you to be there, but I wanted to make sure I was there when you arrived."

Jamie clasped his hand tight, thankful that her uncle was still alive.

"Do you know the deputy's name?" Gavin asked.

Paxton shook his head. "No, he's new to the

area, but he's definitely one of Miller's goons. He demanded I leave with him, and when I tried to get away, he shot me! Then he started to drag me outside, but someone showed up at the back door and he went outside to investigate. I booked it. I managed to make it to where I'd parked the ATV in the woods some distance from the house. I never would have made it out of there on my own steam."

That explained the engine noise Gavin had heard in the woods behind Jamie's house before he ran into the man who'd attacked him.

Gavin remembered the ransacked house and trailer. Had they been looking for the drugs or something more? Perhaps the evidence?

"I was afraid he'd catch up with me before I got here, so I didn't take a direct route. When I was a little ways from here, I hid the ATV and came the rest of the way in on foot. I didn't think I'd make it." He stopped for a breath. "It took me forever to get here. When I did, I found my office torn apart. I figured they'd searched the mine by then and moved on. Miller's goons didn't know about the new additions I'd made." He stared at Jamie. "How did you find me?"

Gavin could see that Jamie was struggling with how to tell her uncle about Terry. He touched her arm. "Let me." She slowly nodded, and Gavin turned to Paxton. "There's something we need to tell you that's going to be difficult to hear. Terry's dead, Paxton. I'm guessing he was the one who showed up at your house. Miller's men probably killed him."

Paxton's mouth fell open in shock. Words wouldn't come for the longest time. "If I'd stuck around, I could have helped him," he finally managed.

"No. If you'd stayed, you'd be dead, as well," Gavin was quick to assure him. "Terry was just at the wrong place at the wrong time."

"Poor Terry." Paxton wept with grief. "He was only trying to help me. He's been helping me all along."

Jamie gathered her uncle close until he was able to talk again.

"We saw the heroin. How did it get here?" she asked.

Paxton appeared shell-shocked. It was a little bit before he could answer. "I saw where the deputies were storing it, and Terry and I took it one night. We knew we had to find a way to stop them. They just kept bringing the stuff into the county. It was killing our community and our kids. Their future. I couldn't let that happen any longer."

"How did you get all the evidence you gathered?" Gavin wanted to know.

Paxton shook his head. "I started working on

that a few years ago. I figured if I stuck with it, I'd find out who was behind the drugs with Terry's help. I had no idea exactly what was going on here until recently." Paxton put his head in his hands. "Oh, Terry. I can't believe he's gone. I did this to him."

Jamie touched his shoulder. "This isn't your fault, Uncle Paxton. They're the ones who killed Terry. Not you."

"This is all because of that guy I saw them with. I found out the former sheriff and most of the deputies are dirty, and I think it's because of that guy."

From everything Gavin knew about the Southern Mafia, they were good at making witnesses disappear. How had Paxton managed to gather so much evidence without anyone realizing he was on to them until now?

"How did you make the connection? These guys are good at covering their crimes."

"It took some doing, but I followed the deputies and got a picture of them with that one guy. The only problem is, I have no idea who he is."

Gavin had been hoping Paxton would have a clue who the man was. He was positive he'd never seen him associated with any of the Southern Mafia captains. "Did you find any evidence connecting all of this to my father's murder?" he asked hopefully.

Gavin could tell from the way Paxton didn't make eye contact that he hadn't. It was gut-wrenching. Part of him wanted to believe in Noah's innocence.

"Not yet, but I overheard Miller talking to one of his goons the day before they showed up at my place. I'd followed him because I knew he was up to no good. Miller was furious about the missing drugs and mentioned that he'd have to take care of me the way they had the last person to stand in their way. That's when I knew they had something to do with Charles's death, so I called Jamie. There's a connection between what happened to Charles and the drugs and I believe it has everything to do with the man I can't identify in the photo. He's responsible somehow."

Paxton might be convinced Miller's comments were a form of a confession, but in Gavin's mind they could mean anything. There wasn't enough evidence to prove anyone else was responsible for his father's death but Noah.

"Do you know how the current sheriff fits into the puzzle?" he asked instead of pointing out the obvious.

Paxton snorted. "Now that one, he's a slippery one. I haven't been able to tie him to any of his deputies' crimes yet. He's good at covering his tracks, but I'm sure he's dirty, just like his father."

Gavin wasn't as convinced. Andy was lots of things, but was he a killer? Right now, the more pressing issue was getting out of the mine before they ran out of air.

Jamie seemed to read his thoughts. "None of this does us any good if we can't get out of here. Paxton, they've blocked the main entrance. Is there another way out?"

Paxton closed his eyes. "I don't know. Let me think." His voice was barely a whisper. He didn't look good.

Jamie placed her hand over Paxton's forehead. She caught Gavin's eye. "He's warm to the touch." She pointed to the blood on his jeans.

"Let me take a look at your leg. I'll need to cut away your jeans," Gavin said. Paxton didn't protest, which was alarming enough. The man didn't like people fussing over him.

Gavin pulled out his pocketknife and ripped the jeans away from the wound. Right away he could see that it was bad. The wound hadn't been treated and was showing signs of infection. "The bullet's still in there," he told Jamie. The news was frightening. "We need to bandage it to make him as comfortable as possible."

Paxton looked to his niece for reassurance. "It'll be okay," she said. "Gavin's going to dress the wound."

After staring at his niece for a long moment, Paxton agreed.

"It looks like it's not so bad," Gavin tried to reassure Paxton. He could see that the man was terrified. "I'll try to be as careful as I can."

"Just do it already," Paxton muttered.

Gavin took out some of the extra strips of cloth and wrapped them tightly around Paxton's wound. The man slumped back on the ground. He'd lost consciousness.

"Paxton!" Jamie shook her uncle with fear in her eyes.

Gavin felt for a pulse. It was weak, but steady. "He's okay. Rest is the best thing for him right now." He sat back on his haunches and tried to come up with a plan to get them out of there.

"We won't be able to stay in here for long. We're running out of air." Gavin took Paxton's light and searched around until he found his phone, then he nodded toward the entrance. "Let's talk out there."

He moved through the hole. Once they were on the other side, Jamie went a little way from it so that Paxton couldn't overhear their discussion if he woke up.

"There has to be another way out. These old mines always have another way out," Jamie said. Gavin knew that wasn't necessarily the truth, but she was hanging on to it and so would he.

"You're right." He looked inside where Paxton slept. "He's okay for the moment. Let's keep going down this passage. If we find a way out, we can come back for him."

Gavin headed down the tunnel they'd been traveling when they found Paxton. Gavin's own strength almost nonexistent. He'd taken some pain medication before they entered the mine, but he knew he couldn't handle much more.

After they'd walked for some distance, the passage suddenly ended and they were met with the stone wall of the mountainside.

They'd reached the end of the mine, and there was no way out from here.

THIRTEEN

Jamie stared at the rock before them and almost lost it. They'd come all this way only to find they were still trapped.

She turned to Gavin. Saw the same despair in his eyes and fought back tears.

"What do we do now?" She forced the words out, her voice clogged with emotion.

For the first time, the man who had been her rock through all of this had no answer. "I don't know." The desolation in his tone scared her more than anything.

"We should probably get back to Paxton." She said the first thing that came to mind because she'd never seen Gavin look so lost before. "He may have woken by now."

Together they turned and headed back to the room where they'd left her uncle. It was frustrating to realize that they were so close to finding the person behind the drug trafficking in Darlan, and yet they might not make it out alive to bring the true killer to justice.

Once they reached the hole in the wall, they went back inside. Paxton still slept fitfully, tossing and turning and mumbling to himself. Jamie sat down next to him and felt his forehead. "He's burning up."

Gavin unzipped his backpack. "The antibiotics and pain medicine. We'll need to get him awake so that he can take them, though." He looked into her eyes. "Jamie, the infection is probably spreading quickly. He needs a doctor, and soon."

Jamie couldn't think about losing Paxton now. She had to keep fighting to save his life. She shook her uncle hard. "Uncle Paxton, wake up. I need you to wake up now."

Paxton moved his head back and forth and continued to mumble. Jamie leaned closer, but couldn't make out what he was trying to say. She shook him again. "Paxton, wake up now."

Suddenly, her uncle yelled at the top of his lungs and pushed her hard. She fell backwards. Shocked, Jamie saw he appeared to be struggling to free himself from an invisible capture.

Jamie scrambled back to him and tried again. "Uncle Paxton, it's me, Jamie. I need you to wake up. You're very sick. You need medicine."

"No, no, you're not going to kill me. You're

not shutting me up. I've fought too hard to clear my brother's name. I'll keep fighting until the day I do. I won't stop now."

"He's delirious," Gavin said with a weary sigh.

Jamie shook her uncle once more. He grew suddenly quiet. This was even more terrifying than the ramblings. She was so afraid she'd lose him.

Then, slowly, he opened his eyes and struggled to focus on her. "Jamie, what are you doing here?" he mumbled, slurring his words.

She motioned to Gavin to hand her the antibiotics and one of the pain pills. "Paxton, we're here to help you. I need you to take this medicine. It will make you feel better." She held it up to his lips. For a moment she was afraid he'd push it away. But then he took the pills and swallowed them. She opened the water bottle and held it up. He took a sip and then slumped back to the ground, his eyes closed.

"We can't let him die down here, Gavin," she whispered. "The antibiotics will help the infection, but he's in bad shape."

Gavin's expression was grave. "Stay here with him. I'm going to try to backtrack to the spot where the mine collapsed. Maybe we missed something that direction. It's worth a shot."

He started to get to his feet, but she reached for his hand, stopping him. "Be careful."

Regret filled his eyes. Had he been expecting more from her? She cared about him, always would, but he still believed her father responsible for taking Charles's life. They were on opposite sides of something that appeared to be about as insurmountable as the mountain surrounding them.

Gavin rose to his feet, shoving aside the remorse that tore at his heart. "I will be. Keep an eye on this guy." He grabbed his Glock and tucked it behind his back. "Keep the shotgun close. If you hear anything suspicious, shoot first, ask questions later."

She smiled at his attempt at humor. "I will."

Gavin slipped through the hole again. With one final look at Jamie, he headed back the way they'd come.

They still had no idea why the deputies were involved in smuggling drugs into Darlan. It went against everything he believed in. His gut told him Miller and the rest of his goons were committing the crime without the knowledge of their sheriff. Yet how could Andy not know what was happening right under his nose?

None of it made sense. They were missing a crucial piece of evidence, and without it, they might never figure out who was really behind the operation.

Gavin reached the point where the passage-way he was on split from the original one. His side throbbed. Every breath he took became more labored. Their air supply was evaporating. He had to find a way out. There was no other option to save their lives.

The second tunnel that they hadn't explored loomed before him. He was all out of options. It was this or nothing.

Something captured his attention—what sounded like voices, just past where the mine had collapsed. He eased closer.

"This is the last of it, but there's still a whole lot more unaccounted for." Gavin recognized the voice of Dan Miller.

"You think the rest is farther in the mine?" another familiar voice asked.

"I wouldn't put it past that old coot," Miller said in disgust. "With the thing collapsed, I don't see a way to get to it."

"You're right. It will take days, if not weeks, to dig through that rubble. How are we going to explain it to him?"

Silence followed. For once it seemed as if Miller didn't have an answer. "You leave that to me," he snapped. "First thing we need to do is get this stuff to a safe location. We can't afford to lose any more product. He's coming in today, and he won't be happy with the way things have gone. That crazy old fool." The words were spat out. "Why couldn't he have left well enough alone? His brother's dead, anyway. Nothing he found out will clear his name or bring the man back."

Gavin froze. Was Miller admitting he knew something more about Charles's death?

"I need to talk to Sheriff Lawson. Find out what he wants to do here. Come on. Let's get out of here. I never did understand why someone would choose to do this for a living."

Stunned, Gavin couldn't move. Miller had just confirmed that Andy was the leader of the drug smuggling outfit. He'd been wrong. Gavin just couldn't believe it. There had to be something more he was missing.

With time running out, he eased back to the second tunnel. It was quite a bit narrower than the one they went down before. It looked much less stable, as if it had been years since anyone had been that way.

He started walking. The light from his flash-light app revealed decay all around. In several places, the rocks had slid from the walls and almost blocked the way. In spots there was barely room enough to crawl around piles of rocks.

He walked until he reached the spot where the tunnel had been boarded up, and he struggled to keep the despair away.

"Lord, I sure could use Your help now."

Gavin shone the light through the gaps in the boards. The passage didn't appear damaged beyond this spot. Why had someone boarded it up? He had to find out.

With only his hands, he yanked at the first board. It freed easily enough. The second did the same. It was almost as if someone had put them up for appearances only.

Once he'd cleared the passage, Gavin stepped over the remaining boards and headed down the tunnel. Nothing about it appeared any different from the way he'd come. Was he wasting what little time he and Jamie had left? If they were going to die down here, he wanted every moment to count.

Something he couldn't explain urged him on. He couldn't give up now. Jamie was counting on him.

After he'd gone a little way, he spotted more rocks piled up and almost lost hope. Dropping to his knees in front of the rocks, he wasn't sure how much longer he could go on. He gathered his waning strength, and started shoving rocks aside. Behind him, he could hear stones falling. The passage was unstable. If it collapsed on itself, Jamie and her uncle would be trapped inside, and he would have no way to dig them out.

He'd moved more than a dozen large rocks,

when he felt it. Fresh air rushed in. He'd found a way out!

Gavin worked harder. When the last rock was out of the way, he stepped out into the darkness, breathing in clean mountain air. He had no idea where the opening let out, but it didn't matter. They had a chance. He killed the flashlight and listened. Not a sound beyond the normal mountain noises.

He needed to get them help right away, and at this point there was only one person he trusted. Gavin dialed the number for his Scorpion commander, Jase Bradford. He didn't have to wait long.

"Hey, buddy, how are you holding up?" Before he'd left for Darlan, Gavin had told his commander and good friend all about his plucky grandmother, yet he'd never been able to tell anyone, not even Emily, what had happened to his father.

"Not so good." Gavin quickly updated Jase on what they'd been through.

"Sounds like we need to get the FBI involved in this. I'll call the Louisville branch and get them on their way."

Thank You, God. Gavin's knees went weak with relief.

"I appreciate it, Jase. I should go. I need to

get Jamie and Paxton out of here while we still have the chance."

"Be careful," Jase warned. "These guys are cops, and we don't know how far up the food chain the corruption goes. Get out of there before the whole thing collapses on top of you, and get some place safe. Do you have any idea where the opening is located?"

"Hang on." Gavin had an app installed on his phone that gave him the latitude and longitude coordinates. Once he had them, he gave them to Jase.

"Good. I'll pass this on to the FBI. Leave your phone where it has service. I'll have them track you from there. I'll be praying for you, my friend," Jase told him.

"Thanks." They'd need all the prayers they could get. Gavin ended the call with a small amount of hope. Someone knew where they were. He'd trust his commander to bring them help. Right now, he had to get Jamie and Paxton out of the mine before the only way out was gone.

Leaving the phone on a rock outside, Gavin hurried back through the entrance and down the unstable tunnel once more while rubble continued to fall around him. The place was in bad shape. The earlier collapse hadn't helped it much.

Please don't let it come down, Lord. It's our

only means of escape. Bring us out of this thing safely, he prayed fervently.

Once he was back in the main passage, he looked behind him. Pieces of rocks continued to fall.

With his heart in his throat, he ran back to the passage he and Jamie had taken. Picking up any speed at all was difficult, as he had to bend over the entire way. Fresh air rushed through the mine. At least they wouldn't suffocate.

What if he got them both back to this point, only to have the mine collapse? They'd be buried alive with no way out.

FOURTEEN

Gavin had been gone for almost two hours. Throughout each of those hours, Jamie's uncertainties had continued to grow. Paxton seemed to be resting a bit more peacefully, but he still hadn't regained consciousness.

Several times, she'd heard rumblings from the direction that Gavin had gone. She had no doubt in her mind that the mine was quickly becoming more unstable. There had already been one collapse; others might follow. The mine could be filling with dangerous gases. She'd never felt so helpless.

A noise coming from nearby sent her jumping to her feet. She hurried to the wall closest to the opening as footsteps grew closer. Was it Gavin? She couldn't afford to take any chances.

Someone stepped inside the room. "That's far enough," she said and pointed the shotgun at the intruder.

"Jamie, don't shoot. It's me." Gavin's husky voice had never been more welcome.

She dropped the weapon and ran into his arms. "I was so afraid the place would collapse."

He held her close for a moment then looked down at her and smiled. "I've found a way out."

Her eyes grew large. "You did? That's great."

"While I was outside, I called my commander. He's getting in touch with the FBI. Help is on the way."

There was more, she could tell. "What aren't you telling me?"

He let her go and stepped away. "The opening is located in a part of the mine that's very unstable. We don't have much time. We need to get out of here now before our only means of escape goes away."

She glanced down at Paxton. "We can't leave him behind."

He clasped her hand. "No, of course not. We'll try to wake him. Otherwise, we'll have to carry him, and I'm not sure I'm up to it or if we have that much time. Has he been awake at all?"

Jamie shook her head. "At least he's sleeping a bit more peacefully." She went over to where her uncle lay. "Paxton, wake up." She shook him hard. He winced in pain before slowly opening his eyes.

"What happened?" His voice was barely audible.

"We're getting out of here. Gavin found a way out, but the mine is unstable. Do you think you can walk?"

Paxton managed a nod and then slowly sat up, closing his eyes briefly. He put his hand up to his head. "I think I'm going to need some help."

Gavin came around to one side. With Jamie on the other, they lifted him to his feet.

"Can you put any weight on your injured leg?" Gavin asked.

Paxton tried to stand on the leg. He screamed in pain and almost dropped to the ground.

"We'll help you," Jamie assured him.

"Let me get on the other side, and I can get him through the entrance," Gavin said.

Jamie put her arm around Paxton's waist, and he leaned heavily against her as Gavin slipped through the opening.

"You're going to have to put some weight on your injured leg, but we'll make it quick," Gavin told him.

With Jamie still holding on to her uncle, he slowly put his full weight on the leg. Jamie could tell it was a struggle to keep from losing his balance. The extent of the pain was carved on his face as he eased through the opening and fell against Gavin's injured side. Gavin stumbled backward and almost lost his footing.

Jamie hurried through the opening and grabbed

Paxton around the waist again, taking some of the weight off Gavin.

"Are you okay?" she asked with concern.

Gavin managed a nod, his jaw tight. She knew he was hurting.

"I think so. Let's get going. This will take a while, and I'm not sure how long we have."

With Gavin's arm touching hers, together they carried Paxton down the narrow passage. The going was slow and strenuous, forcing them to stop periodically to catch their breaths. Gavin was barely hanging on himself. She wasn't sure how much more he could handle.

"We're almost there. It's not much farther." Gavin tried to sound positive, but she could tell it was a struggle for him to put one foot in front of another.

"I heard Miller talking to one of his men. They got the drugs out of here, but they're looking for more. They think they're hidden inside the mine somewhere. I believe they'll come back here soon to look for them. We can't let them find us."

Jamie couldn't believe it. "How much drugs do you think there are? Paxton, do you have any idea?"

Her uncle was barely conscious, but he managed to answer. "There's plenty, from what I've seen. The amount of heroin they're moving into the county is massive."

Paxton's words were terrifying.

"There's more," Gavin said, and she forced herself to concentrate. "I heard Miller talking. Looks like I was wrong about Andy Lawson. He's not only involved, he's the leader."

Shocked, Jamie stared up at him. "Just how deep does this thing go?"

Gavin stopped once they reached the entrance to the shaft leading to the opening. "This is it."

Jamie peered into the decay and shivered. He couldn't blame her. Nothing about the place looked safe.

"I know it looks bad, but it's not much farther to the opening."

Jamie nodded in spite of the fact that she looked ready to drop. The three of them headed down the narrow passage. With each step they took, pieces of the wall continued to crumble away.

"Do you know where this will put us out?" Gavin asked Paxton, hoping to get Jamie's mind off the danger around them.

"I'm guessing we're on the opposite side of the mountain, not too far out of Darlan." Gavin was amazed at the older man's spunk, in spite of his physical condition.

Behind them, several large rocks split from the side and hit the ground hard. The vibration shook the place, sending tremors down the shaft.

"Hurry, this whole place could go at any moment. Run, Jamie!" Gavin yelled and together they ran for the opening.

They'd almost cleared it when a loud rumble behind them quaked the place. Gavin lost his footing, and Paxton fell to the ground with him.

"Gavin!" Jamie screamed.

Gavin scrambled to his knees. "Help me get him outside," he managed while holding his side. The pain was unbearable.

Jamie got him to his feet. Together, they hauled Paxton up and ran as fast as they could. They barely made it out before the tunnel collapsed onto itself, and a rush of dust and debris flew past them.

Gavin dropped Paxton to the ground and fell to his knees. They'd come so close to being trapped. A few seconds more and they'd all have been dead.

Thank You for bringing us safely out. He murmured the prayer, then stared back at the tomb they'd escaped.

Jamie knelt next to him and touched his face. The tenderness in her eyes gave him strength.

"How are you holding up?" she asked.

He knew she was worried about his injury, but truth be told, he was barely keeping it together.

Gavin smiled so that she wouldn't keep worrying. "Hanging in there. We can't afford to stay here, though. Somehow or other we need to get as far away from here as we can before Miller and his people come back to look for the drugs."

He could tell she didn't believe him about being all right, but what choice did they have? If they stayed here, they'd be dead. "You're right." She turned to Paxton, who looked much worse after the harrowing journey they'd just faced. "What is the easiest way out of here?"

Paxton scrubbed a hand over his eyes and scanned the dark horizon. "There's only one way out, and it's all downhill."

Gavin dragged in a breath and prayed for the strength to finish the job. He spotted his phone where he'd left it on the rock and pocketed it. "Then we'd best get going. We have one thing working in our favor. If they come this way and see the rubble, they'll believe we're trapped inside. It might buy us time. It's something." He struggled to stand. Jamie grabbed him around the waist and helped him up.

"Deep breaths," she whispered close to his ear. "We'll take it slow. We'll be okay."

He looked down at her. Even in the darkness, he could see her reassuring smile. She was trying hard to remain positive. He needed to do the same.

He touched her face. "You're right. We will be." He turned to Paxton. "You know this mountain like the back of your hand. Keep us on the right track."

Together, he and Jamie helped Paxton to his feet.

"How are you feeling?" Gavin asked the older man.

Paxton wasn't one to look for sympathy. "Okay. You got any more of those pills you gave me earlier? I think I could use some now."

Gavin dug into the backpack and brought out the antibiotics, along with the pain medicine. "Here, take one of each of these. It'll help with the pain."

Once Paxton was finished, he handed the water bottle back to Gavin, who swallowed something for his own pain.

"I'll need my light," Paxton told them. Gavin had no idea where the light had ended up.

"I have it." Jamie took it from her jacket pocket.

Paxton put the light on and shone it around the area. He pointed off to their right. "We'll head out that way. It should be the easiest path."

Gavin nodded. "Okay, let's get going." Gavin reached to help Paxton, but the older man pushed his hands away.

"I don't need any help. Hand me that stick over there." He pointed to a log lying close by. "I'll use it to help me along. You two need to watch your footing. It's steep through here. We don't need any more injuries."

Jamie cast a doubtful look Gavin's way. "Are you sure, Uncle Paxton?"

The older man nodded. "I'm sure. Let's head out."

"I'll take the lead," Gavin told them, half expecting Paxton to argue. Shining the light down in front of them, he could see that Paxton was right. The hike was going to be a steep downhill process.

Just put one foot in front of the other.

With Paxton between them, he and Jamie started walking. Miller's words from earlier troubled him.

His brother's dead, anyway. Nothing he found out will clear his name or bring the man back.

Had Paxton been right all along? Had Miller inadvertently let slip that there was something more going on with Charles's murder than what the sheriff's department had reported?

FIFTEEN

A rock rolled beneath her feet and Jamie almost lost her footing. Gavin rushed to her side to steady her.

"Are you okay?" he asked. The alarm on his face warmed her inside.

When her heart finally stopped thundering in her ears, she answered. "Yes, I think so. It's just hard to see where I'm going."

"It is, but Paxton was right. We can't afford another injury. Why don't you use your phone's flashlight app to watch the ground? If they're out there looking for us, they'll spot three lights just the same as they would two."

She dug her phone out of her pocket and clicked on the light.

"Ready?" he asked, and she forced a smile.

"Yes, I'm ready."

As they picked their way down the mountainside, Jamie found herself jumping at every noise around them. She didn't doubt for a moment that Miller would keep looking for them. He wouldn't be satisfied until he knew for certain they were dead. Too much was at stake. In spite of what Gavin believed, she was positive when they found their mystery man, they'd find out who really killed Charles.

Her mind went back over the things they knew so far. Making sense of it was impossible. There was no way Miller was the mastermind behind the organization. As hard as she tried, she couldn't see Andy Lawson running such a huge endeavor, either.

"Who do you think is really in charge?" she asked Gavin, voicing her doubts about Andy. Up ahead, the path widened enough so that she could walk next to Uncle Paxton. She knew he was still in a lot of pain, but using the stick as a crutch seemed to be helping.

"If you're suggesting that Andy doesn't seem capable of such a huge endeavor, I agree. Paxton, in your surveillance photos, I saw a picture with our mystery man along with Miller and some of the other deputies. It looked like it was taken in an abandoned warehouse. Do you remember what that was?"

"That's the equipment storage building for the old mine near Hallettsville. I followed Miller and his goons there one night."

Jamie recalled the photo. The man had been

dressed nicely, in a suit and tie. "I'm guessing he's the real person in charge."

"That's my guess, too," Gavin told her. "We need to figure out who he is and how he's connected to all of this as soon as possible, but first we need to get out of danger."

"How soon before the FBI arrives?" Jamie wasn't sure how much more any of them could take.

Gavin shook his head. "I'm not sure. Maybe a couple of hours. It looks like we're almost at the base of the mountain." He pointed up ahead, and Jamie noticed that the ground was slowly leveling off.

"Can we stop for a moment to rest?" She was out of breath and couldn't imagine how Uncle Paxton must be feeling.

She flashed her light around and spotted a rock big enough for sitting, and helped Paxton over to it.

"Which way from here?" she asked her uncle.

He looked around the countryside he'd grown up exploring. "Best I figure, we're about five miles from town. I'd say we want to avoid that. There's an abandoned homestead not too far from here. We could hide out there until the Feds show up."

The thought of being inside sounded wonderful to Jamie. "Good idea. Hopefully, they won't look for us there."

"Let's get going then. God helps those who help themselves, I say." Paxton shuffled to his feet, and she chuckled at her uncle's bravery. In so many ways, he reminded her of her father. Always seeing the positive side of things. Never wanting to lean on anyone. Her father was a pillar of strength in her mind. Even today, she couldn't reconcile what she knew about him with the frail man he'd been before his death.

Uncle Paxton led the way. Soon, she spotted the house up ahead of them. As they headed toward it, Jamie couldn't shake the bad feeling growing inside of her. Who was the well-dressed man in the photo, and why had he met with Miller? There was something more going on here than they knew. She just had no idea what.

As they drew close to the house, Gavin stopped suddenly, as if something wasn't right.

She halted next to him. "What is it?"

He pointed to the ground. "If this place is abandoned, then why are there tire tracks here?"

Jamie had barely had time to look down when from behind the barn, four ATVs fired their engines and headed for them at breakneck speed.

"Run for the woods behind the house," Gavin told her. Together, they grabbed Paxton around the waist and hurried for the trees. Before they'd managed even a handful of steps, one of the men began shooting at them.

"Get down." Gavin shoved her and Paxton behind an abandoned car then took out his weapon and returned fire.

Jamie eased next to him with the shotgun. All four ATVs had their lights on bright and directed right at them. He glanced behind them. The woods were close. If they could make it there, they might have a chance at getting away.

"Can you get Paxton to the woods?" Gavin asked while keeping a careful eye on the ATVs. "I can try to hold them off for a while."

Jamie peered behind them. "I think so, but I'm not leaving you behind."

He looked into her eyes. "I'll be right behind you, I promise. Head there as fast as you can. I'll see if I can get them on the retreat." Jamie hated leaving him behind. She cupped his face, holding his gaze. "Please be careful."

He covered her hand with his and smiled. "I will."

She slowly nodded, then took hold of Uncle Paxton and ran as fast as she could for the tree coverage. Behind her, Gavin opened fire.

"We're almost there," she urged her uncle, trying to sound positive. Even though just a handful of steps now separated them from the woods, it felt like miles with the firefight going on behind them.

They reached the edge of the trees. Behind them, Jamie heard footsteps. Gavin was running their way through heavy gunfire.

Please keep him safe, she prayed. She couldn't bear the thought of something happening to Gavin.

Jamie barely made it to the first tree before she bumped into Paxton. Why had he stopped?

"Hurry, Uncle Paxton. We have to keep moving."

Paxton didn't answer. He was staring at something in front of him.

It took only a second before her eyes adjusted to the darkness and she spotted what he saw. Two men stood close with weapons aimed at them. They'd walked straight into a trap.

Gavin rushed for the trees behind the house. He spotted Jamie and Paxton right away. Something was off.

"What's wrong?" He barely got the words out when a set of flashlights clicked on, blinding him.

He recognized the first man: the former sheriff of Darlan County, Raymond Lawson. The man standing next to him Gavin had seen before, as well, in a photo. It was their mystery man.

Reality slammed into place. They'd fought so hard to get free of the mine, only to be captured by the men who put them there.

"Well, well, we have all three of you right here in one place." The mystery man stopped a few feet short of them and turned back to Lawson. "Good job, sheriff."

Who was this man? If they were going to die at his hands, Gavin had to know his true identity. "So, you're the man behind the heroin. I never did believe Miller and the rest of his men were smart enough to run an organization this size by themselves."

The mystery man looked at Gavin with admiration. "Oh, I don't know. Sheriff Lawson here has run the operation for me quite nicely through the years. But you're right. I am the man behind the heroin. And I can see you don't know who I am."

Gavin was immediately on alert. Why would he say that? "Should I?"

A smirk followed. "Your father surely would."

The truth dawned on him slowly. "How do you know my father?" But the ball in the pit of his stomach told him he knew the answer. This was the man who'd killed Charles. The true killer. Jamie had been right all along. Reality mingled with guilt threatened to buckle his knees.

"I was the last man to see him alive, Agent Dalton."

The truth threatened to sink him. Jamie must have sensed it, because she took his hand.

He forced back rage. "You killed my father." It all became clear. This man was with the mining corporation that had wanted to buy out his father's mine.

The man smiled. "That's right. I needed the mine. He refused to sell. He had to die."

It took everything inside Gavin not to charge the man. He wanted him dead for murdering his father. "You wanted the mine because of its central location." It was a shot in the dark, but the man's expression slipped a little, confirming Gavin was right. "It's close to the other abandoned mines you've bought out, and it would allow you easy access out of town. I guess you didn't count on my grandmother not automatically selling the business to you after my father's death."

Paxton made a noise that sounded like disbelief. "You're part of Shadow Mining," he exclaimed.

The man didn't seem worried that they'd discovered his identity. He clearly wasn't planning to let them live. "Not part of it. I'm the owner of Shadow Mining. Brock Shadow."

The name didn't ring any bells for Gavin. "You had one of your goons put pressure on Paxton here to force my grandmother to sell, thinking them both easy targets. When you couldn't get Paxton to cooperate, you tried to kill him, too."

Three of the men who'd been shooting at them came up behind and started to grab them, but Shadow stopped them. "Leave them alone. We'll take care of them soon enough."

Gavin tried not to react to the threat. Would help be there in time to save them? "You won't get away with this, Shadow. I'm a CIA agent."

Shadow was unmoved. "Yes, well, mines around here collapse all the time. Especially ones like the Darlan Mountain Mine. It's been neglected for years by Paxton."

The look on Jamie's face reflected her terror. Gavin moved closer, still holding her hand. "If you kill us, how will you find the rest of the drugs?"

Shadow's gaze narrowed, suspecting a lie. "You're stalling. Get his phone," he ordered one of the men. "I want to see who he's called."

One of the men grabbed him while a second searched his pockets, came up with the cell phone and tossed it to his boss.

Shadow scrolled through the recent calls and spotted Jase's number.

"Who's this?" he demanded. "Who did you call?"

Gavin had to come up with a believable answer quickly.

"I've contacted the FBI. They're on their way here now."

Shadow's confidence slipped a little. "The FBI. It will take them hours to get boots on the ground. By then we can be out of here with our product, and you'll be dead." He motioned to the man still holding Gavin, and he shoved him away.

Shadow walked over to Paxton. "Where is the rest of my product, old man?" The anger on his face was easy to read.

Still Paxton didn't back down. "It's gone. I destroyed it. I would have done the same with the stash in the mine if I hadn't run out of time."

Shadow moved to inches from Paxton's face. "You're lying. You still have it somewhere, along with the evidence you've been sneaking around gathering."

That Shadow knew about Paxton's covert actions came as a surprise.

Shadow smiled. "You didn't think I knew? You foolish man. I've had my men keep tabs on you through the years. While you were a potential threat to my empire, everyone in the county thought you were a kook. No one believed you. You were harmless until you decided to steal my heroin. Where's the rest of the evidence? I know there's more."

Paxton's bravado faded a little. "I ain't telling you nothing."

Shadow shook his head in distaste. "It's in the mine somewhere. Get them back there. Find whatever he's been stashing and then get rid of the problem these three pose. For good, this time."

The threat was clear. They were not walking out of the mine alive. Gavin knew he had to do something to buy time for the FBI to reach them before it was too late.

Another deputy appeared behind them. "The mine's unsteady. Another tunnel has collapsed."

This was not the news Shadow wanted to hear. "Then find another way in. We need the heroin before our buyer arrives, and we can't afford to have incriminating evidence left behind for someone to find later on. Understood?"

The deputy frowned at the order. "Yes, sir." He motioned to another deputy. "You heard the man. Let's get going."

Gavin and Jamie were forced from the woods at gunpoint while two men grabbed Paxton and hauled him out, as well.

"Get the old man on one of the ATVs. The others can walk," the deputy ordered.

One of the deputies forced Paxton onto a nearby machine, got on behind him and headed back up to the mine.

A gun barrel was shoved into Gavin's back. "Move it. You two have wasted enough of our time."

Sheriff Lawson and Brock Shadow climbed on separate ATVs, as did another deputy, and followed Paxton up the mountain.

The two remaining deputies forced Gavin and Jamie to keep moving.

Gavin got as close to Jamie as he dared in an effort to protect her.

"How much longer...?" She didn't finish but he understood.

"Soon, I hope." He forced the words out. The guilt he felt at not believing her all these years gnawed at him. She'd needed him and he'd let her down. Jamie deserved someone better than him. He'd do everything in his power to get her safely out of this and then he prayed he'd be deserving of her forgiveness one day.

SIXTEEN

"No talking, you two." One of the men behind them shoved his weapon hard against Gavin's back, sending him stumbling forward. "Keep moving."

Jamie reached out to steady Gavin, who managed to catch himself before he hit the rocky ground.

"Are you okay?" she whispered.

"I said no more talking," the man growled.

Gavin nodded in answer, trying to reassure her.

Jamie grabbed his hand once more. She didn't know what the future held for them, but she was determined to make every second count. She'd hold Gavin's hand as long as she was allowed.

Up ahead, she noticed Sheriff Lawson, Shadow and the others had reached the collapsed tunnel where the three of them had escaped. They were staring at it. It would take days to dig through the rubble.

Once Jamie and Gavin reached them, she could tell Shadow was quickly losing patience.

"Don't tell me there's not another way in there. You're a tunnel rat. You know how to get into that mine. Now tell me where the entrance is."

Paxton clamped his lips together and shook his head.

"Perhaps you'll tell me if she's in enough pain?" Shadow motioned to one of the men behind Jamie. The deputy grabbed her and twisted her arm behind her back.

Right away Gavin charged the man, but the deputy behind him jammed his weapon against Gavin's injured side. He dropped to his knees in pain.

"I can have him keep going if you'd like. Break a few of her bones—or you can talk and save your niece's life."

The man holding Jamie's arm yanked it hard and she screamed.

"That's enough!" Paxton yelled. "Stop hurting her. I'll tell you where the third opening is."

Shadow smiled smugly. "That's better." He nodded to the man grasping Jamie's arm, and he eased up a little.

"Well, where is it?" Shadow demanded. "We don't have all day."

Paxton's gaze met Jamie's. She could see how bad he felt.

"It's okay, Uncle Paxton. Just tell them what they need to know," Jamie urged. She didn't want Shadow to kill him.

He slowly nodded. "It's that way. I made the opening a little while back." The direction he indicated had to be on the opposite side of the tunnel from Paxton's hiding place.

"Get him in there and find the stuff," Shadow demanded in an irritated tone.

The deputy who had ridden with Paxton hopped on the machine again and headed the ATV toward the spot Paxton had pointed out, followed by a second deputy.

"Take them there, too," Shadow told the two deputies guarding Jamie and Gavin. Then he and the sheriff got on their machines and went after her uncle.

"You heard the boss. Get moving." The deputy let Jamie go and shoved her forward.

With Gavin sticking close to her side, they were forced up the rocky slope. Jamie could see Gavin was barely hanging on. They needed God's help now more than ever, and so she prayed with all her remaining strength for deliverance.

It felt as if it took forever to reach the place. Once she and Gavin had caught up with the ATVs, she noticed that Paxton had whittled an opening into the side of the mountain. He'd hidden it well, covering it with scrub brush.

"Get him inside and get the evidence. Find out if he's lying about the heroin. I don't trust him." Shadow gave the order. Two deputies grasped Paxton's arms and dragged him inside.

"What about these two?" Lawson asked. Jamie held her breath. Would they kill them right there?

"Not yet, sheriff. Their time will come."

Jamie's gaze clung to Gavin's. Besides the former sheriff and Shadow, there were two armed deputies standing guard. She didn't like their odds.

Gavin shook his head. The concern in his eyes told her that he agreed. If they tried to overpower the men and failed, they'd be dead before they had the chance to think about it.

As she stared at the gaping hole before them, Jamie couldn't imagine a good outcome. It broke her heart to consider what might have been. She cared for Gavin and she didn't want to lose him. Not like this. *Father, please, we need Your help. Please, don't let us die here when we're so close to the truth.*

The two deputies behind them began talking to each other. Gavin knew he had to try something to save their lives. Shadow and Lawson were watching the entrance. If they went down into that mine again, they'd probably end up with bullets in their heads.

He looked down at Jamie and pointed discreetly at Shadow and Lawson. She swallowed hard before slowly nodding.

Another quick glimpse at Shadow and Lawson proved their attention was still distracted.

Gavin placed three fingers against his chest, slowly counting them off. With his heart in his throat, he charged to where Shadow stood. Jamie did the same. With Shadow caught off guard, Gavin managed to grab the man's weapon and fire off a shot at one of the two deputy's racing at them.

Struck in the knee, he dropped to the ground, screaming in pain.

Jamie grabbed Lawson's weapon and aimed it at the remaining deputy.

"Put the weapon down on the ground. Now," Gavin ordered when the deputy standing made no move to obey.

"Take it easy. I'll do as you ask," the deputy said. He slowly lowered his weapon.

"I've got Lawson covered. Can you get their weapons?" Gavin asked and Jamie hurriedly gathered the two deputies' weapons while Gavin stood watch.

Sheriff Lawson's glare proved he was furious. "You don't know who you're dealing with, Dalton."

"Keep quiet," Gavin ordered, then addressed the standing deputy.

"Help your buddy up and over to that ATV." The man hesitated a second, then hauled the injured man over to the machine. "Now cuff him to the handlebars." Once the deputy had finished, Gavin said to Jamie, "Take the key from the ATV, and then grab the second deputy's cuffs and secure him to that tree over there." Gavin pointed the weapon at the man. "Start moving." The deputy tossed Gavin angry looks as he headed for the tree.

"Wrap your hands around it," Jamie ordered. The man seemed to realize what was happening because he didn't move.

"Do it now, or I start shooting," Gavin said and the man finally obeyed.

Jamie cuffed the man to the tree then searched him and the second deputy, taking their phones and the keys to the handcuffs. She went back over to where Gavin stood guarding the others.

"Get going." Gavin pointed his weapon at the entrance. Lawson and Shadow exchanged a look before obeying.

As they slowly headed into the mine, Shadow

and Lawson whispered between themselves, no doubt scheming how to get away.

"That's enough talking," Gavin told them, and they shut up.

Jamie followed close behind Gavin. "What's the plan?" she whispered so that only he could hear.

He had no idea, only that he was doing his best to buy them time. "Just trying to keep us alive until our help arrives." He kept his voice as low as he could.

As they drew close to the place where the evidence was stored, Gavin stopped while the men kept going. "We'll have to get the other men subdued as quickly as possible. Follow my lead."

Jamie nodded, and they caught up with Shadow and Lawson. They were close to Paxton's hiding place now. He could hear the men who had gone with Paxton talking.

"He has file cabinets filled with this stuff. He must have been collecting it for years." A file cabinet closed.

"They're out here!" Shadow yelled to alert the rest of his men.

Gavin grabbed Shadow around the neck while Jamie kept her weapon against Lawson's back. The second Gavin and Jamie entered the room, they were met with armed men drawing down on them.

"I wouldn't do that if I were you," Gavin told them and tightened his grip on Shadow. "Not if you want your boss to live."

The men hesitated, glancing at each other as if trying to decide what to do.

"Shoot them both," Shadow ordered.

"Drop your weapons if you want him to live," Gavin said in a steely tone, unlike what he felt inside. His heart pounded in his ears. They were outnumbered. He was praying the men would buy his bluff.

"Don't do it. Shoot them!" Shadow yelled.

Gavin pushed the Glock against Shadow's temple. "Tell them to lay down their arms now."

The man standing close to one of the file cabinets slowly lowered his weapon to the ground.

"Kick the weapon this way and get your hands in the air," Gavin told him.

The man obeyed. The second man shoved his gun against Paxton's side. "I'll shoot him."

Paxton was barely hanging on after the exertion of walking back through the mine. Gavin could see the fear in the older man's eyes.

"No, you won't. Drop the weapon or I'll kill your boss."

The man stared at Shadow, uncertain what to do.

"Do it now." Gavin dug the gun into Shadow's temple.

The man lowered his weapon.

"Now step away from him." He pointed his weapon toward the other man. "Over there."

The man tossed Gavin an angry look, doing as he requested.

Gavin released his hold on Shadow. "You and Lawson get over there, as well."

Shadow straightened his coat and walked over to his men.

"What do you expect to do now, Dalton?" Shadow demanded, not showing any fear.

"Now we wait for the FBI to show up and throw you and your pals in jail."

Shadow turned his anger on Paxton. "You old coot. You could have been rich beyond your wildest desire if you'd sold the mine when we came to you. None of this would be happening now if you'd stayed out of our way. And the old lady would still be alive."

"You killed Ava?" Paxton asked in disbelief.

But Gavin barely registered the shock in Paxton's voice. His legs threatened to give out beneath him. "You killed my grandmother?"

Shadow showed no emotion at all. "I didn't kill her, I simply went to visit her to try and talk some sense. Only she wouldn't listen to reason. Instead, she got herself all worked up. She figured out I was the one who had her son killed and she started screaming at me and threatening to call her grandson. Then, she just collapsed." Shadow shrugged as if it were nothing. "It was her own fault."

Gavin's thoughts fractured. Shadow might not have killed Ava, but he was the cause of her heart attack. If he'd called for help, Ava might still be alive.

"You murdered Ava because she wouldn't sell to a crook like you who's bent on destroying Darlan County," Paxton said. "You let my brother take the blame for your dirty work."

Shadow smirked in disdain at Paxton's anger, then looked behind him at his men. "What does he have on me?"

"Everything," one of the men answered. "He knows about the heroin. Your dealings with Lawson here."

Shadow turned back to Gavin. "Well, then, I'd say he doesn't know everything yet."

Gavin tried to figure out what Shadow hadn't told him. "We may not know everything, but we do know enough to put you away for a very long time."

Shadow laughed and looked at something just behind Gavin's shoulder.

Before Gavin had time to react, he heard Jamie's shocked gasp. Then someone shoved her toward Paxton. He whirled around, only to have an object slam against the side of his head. He dropped to the ground, his vision blurred, as a set of boots walked past him and kicked his weapon out of reach.

Someone stooped next to him. The last thing he was aware of was Dan Miller's face grinning down at him.

SEVENTEEN

Jamie knelt next to Gavin with tears in her eyes and hope fading.

"Get him inside. We have to gather all these files and leave here as soon as possible. I don't want to take a chance of some of this incriminating information surviving the blast." She barely registered Shadow's order before someone hauled her to her feet and shoved her over to where Paxton sat.

Still unconscious, Gavin was dragged close to them and dropped. Jamie immediately knelt next to him, cradling his head in her lap.

As she watched, the men gathered the information Uncle Paxton had stored there and headed out of the mine.

Shadow stared down at her before delivering their fate. "Make sure the rest of the drugs aren't here and then blow the mine. There's not much time. Our clients will be expecting us to fulfill our end of the deal…otherwise it won't be good for us."

Jamie had no idea what Shadow was talking about. "You're not going to get away with this. The FBI knows we're here. If we end up dead, they'll come after you."

Miller came back with explosives in his hand. "This should do the trick."

She stared at the dynamite in horror as Miller placed it close to the entrance. Jamie knew she had to try to do everything she could to postpone the explosion.

"Who are you working for, Shadow?"

At her shot-in-the-dark guess, Shadow turned back and stared at her in shock.

"What makes you think I'm working for anyone?" he demanded.

"Because there's no way you managed to get that much heroin on your own. You're working with Ericson."

Shadow stared at her for a second longer, then chuckled. "You're smart, girl, I'll give you that. I am working for someone big. Jacob Ericson and you obviously know he's the boss of the Southern Mafia. But that's all about to end. You see, Ericson has served his purpose. He got me the connections to the heroin. Supplied the means of moving it through all the right counties, thanks to having a whole lot of law enforcement on his payroll. Now it's my turn to be in charge."

Shadow watched as Miller continued to place the dynamite in several strategic locations.

"Oh, and Paxton, you should know your friend Terry sold you out. He was working for me, keeping an eye on you. He was supposed to give me something useful to get rid of you once and for all, but he failed to deliver. He had to die."

Paxton lunged for Shadow. "That's a lie. Terry wouldn't do that to me."

Shadow grinned smugly at Paxton's reaction. "He did. He would have sold his soul for the amount of money I offered him. Your friendship, well, I guess it didn't mean as much to him as you thought."

Once the explosives were in place, Shadow and his goons prepared to head out.

Shadow looked directly at Jamie. "So long, Ms. Hendricks. It's too bad you had to find out the truth like this, but at least you know your father wasn't responsible for his friend's death. That should be some comfort to you before you die."

With those chilling words, Shadow left them to their deaths.

Jamie watched Uncle Paxton. She could see how hard he was taking the news of his friend's betrayal. Yet now was not the time for emotions.

"Uncle Paxton, we have to get out of here. If those explosives go off this close, we'll die." Her words finally got through to him.

She looked down at the man lying unconscious close to her.

"Gavin, wake up. We've got to get out of here." She shook him as hard as she could, and he slowly opened his eyes, staring up at her confused.

"What happened?" he mumbled. He touched his head and winced in pain.

"They wired the place with explosives. We have to get as far away from here as we can."

Gavin stumbled to his feet with Jamie helping him. He leaned against her for a second longer, then together they grabbed hold of Paxton and hurried from the room, running as fast as they could down the dead-end tunnel.

Jamie couldn't see anything but darkness. With her heart in her throat, she kept running.

Her phone. She still had it in her pocket. She took it out, illuminating their way.

Up ahead, the end of the passage came into view. Would it be far enough away from the blast to save them?

"Hurry, we have to get as far away from the blast area as we possibly can," Gavin said, struggling to keep up. He'd been through so much over the past few days. She wasn't sure how much more he could take.

"Keep fighting, Gavin. Please, you can't give up." She tightened her grip on Uncle Paxton, trying to take some of the weight off Gavin.

They were just short of the end of the passage when the blast ripped through the tunnel behind them.

Jamie looked back. A cloud of smoke boiled toward them.

"Get down! Face away from the blast!" Gavin yelled, but there was no time.

The world around them shook like an earthquake was ripping through the area. Rocks and other debris flew past.

The blast flung them through the air. Jamie landed hard against the side of the tunnel. She screamed in pain and slid to the ground. It was a struggle to keep from passing out. The strength of the blast embedded bits of rock into her flesh.

As the world around her spun, she struggled to breathe through the dust-clogged air. Each inhalation was excruciating. And it felt as though she'd cracked a few ribs when she slammed into the stone wall.

When the world finally cleared, Jamie glanced around, trying to locate Gavin and Paxton. Her uncle was close, a few feet away. She leaned over and shook him. He moaned pitifully.

Gavin had taken the brunt of the explosion. Right before the blast, he'd pushed her and Paxton in front of him. She saw him and scrambled over. He wasn't moving.

"Gavin!" she screamed in horror and then leaned close. "Gavin, please be alright. Please don't die on me." She was in love with him and she couldn't bear the thought of having to live without him.

He could hear her calling him. She sounded so far away. His body felt glued to the ground. Somehow, he managed to move his arm. Pain ripped through his body and took his breath away. He'd cracked several ribs.

"Gavin, wake up!" Jamie still sounded far away, and yet someone was shaking him. He moaned as the agony caught up with him.

"Oh, Gavin, you're hurt." He could hear the tears in her voice, and he forced his eyes open. Jamie wasn't far away; she was leaning over him, tears spilling down her face. His heart broke. She was worried about him.

"I'm okay. Just a little banged up." He reached up and brushed the tears from her face.

She leaned down and kissed him with all her heart. "I thought I'd lost you."

Gavin pulled her closer and kissed her again.

He was alive. So was she. They might not have much time left, but they were alive for now.

She held him tight. "I'm so glad you're okay," she whispered against his lips.

He smiled against her mouth. "Me, too. Now let's see if we can find a way out of here."

With her help, he managed to sit. Every move he made hurt like crazy and drained his pitiful strength.

Gavin leaned against her, and she held him close. "It's okay. Take your time," she whispered near his ear.

He closed his eyes until the world righted itself. "Is Paxton okay?"

Jamie stared behind them. "I think so."

Gavin saw the man lying on the ground, mumbling to himself. It was hard to see much in the sooty darkness. How much space did they have? If they could figure that out, they'd know how much air supply was left.

Jamie shone the phone's flashlight around. What he saw was disturbing. They were enclosed in a small space. Keeping the panic at bay was hard, but he tried, for Jamie's sake.

She clamped a hand over her mouth, seeing what he did. "Oh, Gavin, what are we going to do?"

He put his arm around her. "We wait. The FBI should be here any moment. They know we're here. It's only a matter of time before they get to us." It wasn't exactly the truth. The FBI would be expecting them to leave the area, and they'd be tracking his phone. It was with Shadow. Would the FBI turn their search that way? If so, he, Jamie and Paxton would be dead soon.

Gavin looked into her eyes and tried to be strong for her. "We just have to stay alive a little bit longer."

She forced a smile, not seeming to believe him.

Paxton stirred and sat up.

"Where are these Feds you've been talking about? Because we all know we won't make it more than a couple of hours with the air supply we have here."

"They should be here anytime." Gavin prayed they would search the surrounding area and not give up on locating them.

"With everything that happened, I almost forgot. Shadow told me he's been working for the Southern Mafia." She recounted what Shadow had said while Gavin was unconscious.

The news settled around Gavin uncomfortably. So it was true. Shadow was planning to take over at the helm of the Southern Mafia? He remembered the recent car bombing in which Ericson's driver was killed.

"He's got to be stopped. He killed your father

and was responsible for Ava's heart attack. We can't let him get away with the crimes he's committed," Jamie said.

She was right, but even if they did manage to somehow get out, how were they going to bring down Shadow when all the evidence Paxton had gathered was gone?

A thought occurred to her. "Each of us can act as a witness. He admitted killing your father to get his mine, and he told me that he worked for Ericson. That has to be enough to arrest him on those charges."

"Plus there are the backup files I left with Ava for safekeeping," Paxton announced calmly, and both Gavin and Jamie turned to stare at him.

"What did you say?" Gavin asked. He wasn't sure he'd heard Paxton correctly.

"I said I have backup files. I left them with Ava. You think I'm foolish enough not to make copies?" Paxton scoffed.

Gavin had looked through most of the stuff at his grandmother's house. He hadn't come across any files. "Do you have any idea where she put them?"

Paxton shook his head. "No, but I gave them to her on a thumb drive small enough to keep in a safe location. She told me she was going to put it someplace no one else would ever look for it.

Obviously, Shadow had no idea she had the evidence otherwise he would have mentioned it."

There was only one place Gavin could think of that she'd hide the drive. But they had to get out of here in order to find it.

The air was still thick with dust particles. Every breath he took reminded him that his last one was getting close. He wasn't going to let Shadow win.

He held up Jamie's phone. "We need to make a video recording of everything that we know...just in case." He looked into her eyes and knew that she understood they might not make it out alive.

EIGHTEEN

A faint scratching noise came from somewhere above them. "Did you hear that?" she asked in amazement.

Gavin studied the ceiling. "I didn't hear anything. What did it sound like?"

Bits of dirt fell to the ground. "Like someone scratching on something."

"Or someone digging…"

Her gaze locked with his. "They're here. The FBI is here."

They had a chance. If they could stay alive long enough for the FBI to rescue them, they had a chance.

"Down here! We're down here!" she yelled as loud as she could.

A few minutes later they heard a response. "It's Sheriff Lawson. I'm going to try to dig you all out. I followed Shadow and the others and saw where they took you. Hang on, I'll see if I can get you of there."

Horror filled Jamie. "Oh, no. Gavin, it's Andy."

Gavin appeared as shocked as she was. He shook his head. "Something doesn't add up. If he's working for Shadow, why would he want to save us?"

"Unless he isn't saving us. Maybe he was sent here to make sure we're dead."

He gathered her close. "The FBI should be here soon. His digging will hopefully give us an air passage, but just in case…"

Gavin took her cell phone that held their recorded messages and hid it behind a rock.

Above them, chunks of rock broke free from the ceiling. They backed away from the spot.

"This place is unstable. It could collapse at any moment." Jamie wondered if that was the sheriff's purpose.

"Andy, hold up. The whole ceiling is about to cave in!" Gavin yelled up at the man.

The digging stopped immediately, and Jamie breathed a sigh of relief. If Andy were trying to kill them, he'd have kept on digging. "He's not working for Shadow."

Gavin nodded. "No, but if he doesn't find a way to get us out of here soon, it won't matter."

The reality of those words washed over her, and she hugged him close. "We need God's help more than ever."

"You're right. Let's pray."

Gavin took her hand. "Father, we need You to guide Andy's hands. Help him find a way out. There are bad people out there intent on hurting others. Please don't let them succeed."

With the prayer, a sense of peace slipped deep inside of her. God was in control. He wouldn't let them die; she truly believed that.

"I've called for backup. Help is on the way. Hang on down there. I'm going to see if I can dig in a different area. At least get you some fresh air coming in. Just to be safe, I need you to get as far away from this side of the tunnel as you can."

"Thanks, Andy!" Jamie called up. She and Gavin tried to help Paxton to the area where the mine had collapsed, but he refused.

"Hang on a minute up there, Lawson." Paxton obstinately stood his ground.

"Uncle Paxton, he's trying to help. If we don't get air in here soon we'll die." She loved her uncle, but he had a stubborn streak a mile wide.

"And I'm telling you I know an easier place to dig," he announced in a gruff tone that had Jamie staring at him in surprise.

"Lawson, if you go to the north wall, there's a crack in the rock there. It should make for easier going, and I don't think the rock is that thick."

"Got it," Andy told them. Jamie could hear

movement outside, and then a few minutes later the digging started again.

The oxygen level in the mine was dwindling with each breath. They had maybe another half hour's worth of air left in the small space. Any amount of exertion was an effort.

Jamie sank down to the ground. Gavin did the same. He tugged her close. She didn't want to die down here like this. Not after she and Gavin had found each other again. She wanted to have a life with him. Wanted to make up for the years they'd lost.

"How long do you think it will take him to get us free?" Jamie asked in a labored voice, because she needed something to hold on to.

"By himself...hours." Her uncle didn't mince words, and the small amount of hope Jamie was holding on to threatened to crumble. There was no way they'd make it that long. Had they come all this way, finally discovered the truth behind Charles's murder, only to take the secret with them to this dusty grave?

Gavin held her close. "But he's not going to be alone for long. The FBI is on their way here now. Don't give up hope, Jamie. We're going to get out of here, and then we're going to bring Shadow and those dirty cops to justice."

As she looked into his eyes, she believed him. She'd fight with everything inside of her to see that they all made it out of the mine alive. Then they'd bring Charles's killer to justice and break up the heroin ring that had Darlan in its grasp once and for all.

Jamie closed her eyes and leaned against his chest, her breathing shallow, like his. They were dying. As hard as Andy tried, he wouldn't be able to free them alone.

He peered around the small space, his thoughts growing fuzzy.

Outside, he heard footsteps and said a grateful prayer. Help had arrived.

Don't let them be too late...

"What are you doing here?" Andy's voice was barely audible through the solid rock.

Gavin strained to hear the answer. When he did, he almost lost all hope. It was Andy's father. "I can't let you do this, son. I can't let you free them. They have to die down there. What they know is too incriminating."

"You're going to shoot me?" Andy asked in amazement, and Jamie stared up at Gavin in horror.

Their last hope would be gone with Andy's death.

"No, you can still walk away from this. Pretend you don't know anything about it," Raymond told his son.

"I can't do that. I've lived with my suspicions about you far too long. I won't let you and Shadow corrupt this county any longer."

The silence that followed was chilling. Then shots were exchanged, and Gavin held Jamie tighter.

When the shots ended, the silence was the most alarming.

If this is Your plan, Lord, then so be it. Gavin wasn't sure he could fight any longer.

"They're here!" Andy called out to them. "The FBI is here and they've brought reinforcements. Hang in there, guys. This is almost over."

Within minutes, heavy equipment could be heard rumbling up the mountainside.

Just the promise that the sound gave roused them.

"Take small breaths. We're going to be okay," Gavin tried to assure Jamie. Paxton was the worse for wear. Gavin noticed that his eyes were shut and he wasn't moving.

Gavin scrambled over and shook him hard. "Stay with me, Paxton. This is almost over. You can't give in yet."

The older man opened his eyes. "I ain't givin' in ever," he mumbled then closed his eyes again.

Gavin left him alone. There was nothing he could do now but keep his prayers going up to God.

He went back over to Jamie. She barely had the strength to open her eyes. "Hey, look at me. Keep looking at me. Keep fighting for me."

She briefly opened them and smiled up at him. He held on to her. He didn't want to lose her like this. Not when they were so close to freedom.

"Agent Dalton, this is Sam Wilson with the FBI. We're going to have to push the rest of the way in. Get as far away as you can from the spot and cover up. We're coming in five."

The only protection they had was a boulder that had dislodged during the explosion. He lifted Jamie in his arms and carried her behind it, then dragged Paxton over. The man mumbled to himself, and Gavin was terrified they'd lose him before they could be rescued.

Once they were all safely behind the boulder, he called out to the agent, "We're as protected as we can get!"

Within seconds, a heavy piece of equipment began pushing against the mountain. Soon, the compromised wall gave way, splintering it into chunks of rock. Fresh air rushed in, and Gavin drew in a lungful. The room around them shook and threatened to collapse. Several men poured into the space.

Gavin struggled to his feet and hauled Jamie

into his arms. She wasn't moving. Was the rescue too late?

"We have to get out of here now. The place is unstable," he told one of the men. "Can you get Paxton out?"

The man nodded, and he and another agent hurried to rescue Paxton.

All Gavin could think about was the woman in his arms. He loved her. He couldn't lose her. Not like this.

Outside, the day had just begun to break. There were agents everywhere. Gavin spotted Andy Lawson kneeling next to a man on the ground. His father. Andy had been forced to take his father's life to save theirs.

An ambulance waited nearby. Gavin hurried toward it. Two EMTs raced for him with a stretcher.

He placed Jamie on it gently. "Help her. Please, don't let her die."

He loved her so much. Never stopped loving her. Now he just had to find a way to be worthy of her.

The two men placed an oxygen mask over her mouth and nose while they took her vitals.

"Her pulse is weak, but she's alive. We need to get her to the hospital right away." A few seconds later, Paxton was brought over. Both he and

Jamie were loaded into the ambulance. Gavin started to get in but one of the agents joined him.

"Sam Wilson. I'm going to have some of my men follow you to the hospital as a precaution. Until Shadow and his thugs are found, you're all at risk."

"Thank you." Gavin was grateful for the protection.

"Don't thank me. Sheriff Lawson was the one who alerted us to where you were buried. If it wasn't for him, we might never have found you in time."

Gavin realized Andy was standing next to the agent. He held out his hand. "Thanks for saving us, Andy. I hate to say it, but I thought you were part of Shadow's team for a while." Gavin stared at the man lying on the ground. "I'm sorry about your father."

Andy swallowed visibly. "Thanks. I've always thought there was something wrong about him, but until I became sheriff, I had no idea how corrupt my dad and the deputies serving him truly were. When I found out the truth, I couldn't let it go on any longer. I had to do something. So I contacted the FBI and told them what I suspected. I just never envisioned this type of outcome."

"We need to go now," one of the EMTs told him, and Gavin nodded, shook Andy's hand and got into the back of the ambulance. His thoughts were fuzzy from the lack of oxygen. He'd leave everything to the FBI for now. He just wanted to be with Jamie.

NINETEEN

Jamie slowly opened her eyes. Her head ached as if someone was banging a sledgehammer inside her brain. When the world focused, she realized she was in a hospital bed. And someone held her hand.

She looked over and saw Gavin, his forehead resting on their joined fingers. He looked as if he was praying.

"Gavin?" she whispered in a croaky voice. Her throat hurt like crazy.

He lifted his head and looked at her. There were tears there. When he saw that she was awake, his face broke into a smile, then he got to his feet and enveloped her in his arms.

"You're awake. I'm so glad." His voice broke with emotion.

Jamie was happy just to be in his arms for the moment. The last thing she remembered was hiding behind the boulder in the mine.

He slowly let her go. "I was so worried about you. So afraid…" He couldn't finish, but she knew.

"I'm okay," she assured him, then she thought about her uncle. "Uncle Paxton?"

"Is fine, as well. He's resting in the next room, heavily guarded and loving every minute of the fact that he was right all along," Gavin told her with a chuckle.

She managed a smile. "When can I see him?"

"Soon. The doctor says the best thing for you now is to rest."

"What about you? How are you doing?"

He grinned down at her. "I'm fine. The doctor took a look my gunshot wound. He wants to remove the bullet, but I told him that would have to wait until this is over."

"Have they found Shadow and his men yet?" she asked.

"Not yet, but the FBI has the whole area saturated with men. All the roads are blocked. It's only a matter of time."

She could see it in his eyes. He wanted to be part of the hunt. With Shadow responsible for his father's death, she didn't blame him. He needed to bring the man down for closure.

"You should go. Bring him in. Make him pay for what he did to your father."

Gavin shook his head. "I don't want to leave

you. It's too risky." He stopped and stared into her eyes with so much pain in his. Jamie believed she knew what was troubling him.

She touched his face. "It's okay. If the tables were turned, I probably wouldn't have believed you either."

His face twisted. "No, you would because that's just who you are. Jamie, I'm so sorry that I didn't do the same for you. You needed me and I let you down."

She shook her head. She didn't want his apology she wanted...his love. Would there be another chance for them?

"You didn't let me down. We were both thrown into an impossible situation. You handled it the best you could." With tears in his eyes, he kissed her fervently and all her hopes for the future they'd once dreamed of took flight once more.

He ended the kiss, but didn't let her go. She'd give anything for this to be finished, but Shadow and his men were still out there.

"I'm safe here. I'm in a hospital room, no doubt surrounded by FBI agents. Go, bring Shadow to justice for Charles."

"Are you sure?" he asked, still reluctant to leave her side.

"I'm sure." She smiled up at him.

Gavin leaned over and kissed her once more. "I'll be back as soon as I can."

Jamie touched his cheek. "And I'll be right here waiting for you."

Gavin brought her hand up to his lips and kissed it, then, with another smile, he left her alone.

Shadow had taken things from her, as well. Her father. The life she could have had with Gavin. The years that Uncle Paxton had fought to bring Charles's true killer to justice. He deserved to pay for his crimes.

But right now, she wanted to see her uncle and thank him for all that he'd done.

Jamie sat up and put her feet on the floor. The effort left her weak. Holding on to whatever she could, she stood and then made her way to the door. Two federal agents stood guard outside.

"Ma'am, I need you to stay inside your room," one of the agents informed her.

"Not until I see my uncle." She stood up straight and didn't budge.

The second agent nodded toward the next room, where two more agents stood outside. "He's in there. Let me help you, ma'am."

The agent took her arm and slowly walked her over to the two guards. They stepped aside, and he opened the door. Once inside, the agent helped her into the chair close to Uncle Paxton's bed.

"Thank you," Jamie said gratefully. The man who'd helped her smiled and left them alone.

Paxton was resting peacefully. She clasped his hand and held it. She was so grateful to him for not giving up through the years when it would have been so easy. Everyone had doubted him, including Jamie.

"There she is." She hadn't realized that Uncle Paxton was awake until he spoke.

She smiled down at her uncle through tears. "Hey, you."

"Where's Gavin?" her uncle asked, his gaze going to the door.

"He was just here, but he left to go help with the manhunt. It's only a matter of time now before Shadow is captured, along with all the crooked deputies. Dad's name will be cleared finally, and we owe it all to you. You never gave up on proving his innocence. He would be so proud of you."

Uncle Paxton smiled up at her. "And you. I know you never doubted his innocence, either. I just wish I could have proven what really happened before he had to die in that horrible place."

Jamie squeezed his hand. "You did everything you could. You fought against so many odds to clear his name."

Her uncle lowered his head. "You and Gavin. You going to marry him?"

Jamie was surprised by the question. "If he'll have me, and I hope he will. I love him so much. I never stopped loving him."

"The feeling is mutual, Jamie. Ava used to tell me all the time that her grandson still loved you. He just couldn't let go of what he believed."

Jamie scrubbed tears from her cheeks. The damage Shadow had done to their families would take a lot of healing to move beyond.

"The past is finally finished. It's time to look toward the future now," her uncle told her. "And I have a confession to make. When I realized that Miller was intent on bringing me in, probably to kill me, I hid the rest of the heroin at the house."

Jamie stared at him. He didn't know about the house yet. "Oh, Uncle Paxton, I'm so sorry. The house… Miller and his men set it on fire. There's nothing left."

Her uncle was shocked by the news. He shook his head. "Those horrible men." He didn't say anything for a moment. "But the heroin wasn't in the house. It's in the plowed land behind the house. I buried it there."

Now Jamie understood why the area had been freshly plowed. It wasn't because Uncle Paxton planned to plant; it was because he'd been hiding evidence.

Suddenly, the lights were extinguished and the room grew dark.

"What's happening?" Jamie could hear the unease in his voice.

"I don't know. I'll check it out." She jumped to her feet and hurried to the door. Two of the agents were still there.

"What's going on?" she asked. The entire floor was dark.

"Go back inside, ma'am. We're checking it out now. We'll figure out what's happening and let you know. Until then, stay inside." The agent pushed her back into the room. Jamie returned to her uncle, who had sat up in bed, his feet hanging over the edge.

"This is his work," he whispered in a fearful voice.

Jamie didn't have to ask who he meant, because she believed the same thing. In spite of a county-wide manhunt, Brock Shadow was coming after them to finish the job.

One of the agents standing guard had offered Gavin the use of their vehicle. He'd been updated on where the hunt for Shadow was situated—an abandoned mine that had been on the list he and Jamie had found.

As much as he hated leaving Jamie, she was

right. He had to see this thing through to the end. He owed it to his father and to Noah.

Gavin drove the ten-plus miles to the mine. There were dozens of law enforcement vehicles parked down from the entrance. Gavin got out of the car and headed toward it. He spotted Andy amongst the group of men standing out front.

Andy came over.

"What's happening in there?" Gavin asked. He wondered why the agents hadn't stormed the mine.

"We tried to get in there, but they fired on us. We have no idea how many of them are in there. Wilson is letting them sweat it for a while longer, and then he's going with a flash grenade. You want to be part of that?"

"Absolutely." It amazed him how well Andy was holding up after being forced to shoot his own dad. "I really am sorry about your father, Andy. I know how hard it is to lose your dad. I can't imagine how difficult it must be under these circumstances."

Andy kept his focus on the activity in front of the mine. "It was. I still can't believe my father was the one who killed yours, acting under Shadow's orders."

Gavin stared at him. He wasn't sure he'd heard him correctly. "What do you mean?"

Andy looked heartbroken. "I learned that my

dad was the one who came to your father originally with the offer. He knew your dad wouldn't accept it. Gavin, my dad went to the mine with Shadow that day. He was the one who shot your dad with a gun he'd taken from Noah's place. Then he lured Noah over to frame him for the murder."

Gavin couldn't believe what he was hearing. "How did you find this out?"

Andy looked at him with regret. "I'm sorry as all get-out about this, Gavin. I found out because one of the deputies who worked for my dad was captured trying to leave the county. I guess the rats are jumping ship. Anyway, he thought he could help himself on his sentence if he started talking."

"Unbelievable." Gavin couldn't imagine how difficult it must be for Andy to admit that not only had his father been corrupt, he was a murderer, as well.

"Looks like they're about to start," Andy told him, and they headed to the entrance.

"Once the flash grenades go off, we'll have only a few minutes' advantage. Be prepared. They have nothing to lose," Agent Wilson told the group.

Seconds after the flash grenades were thrown into the mine, the agents stormed it.

The chaos that Gavin saw when he entered reminded him of many of the war-type situations he'd faced abroad.

Gavin spotted at least five deputies stumbling around. The grenade would make vision impossible for several seconds as well as cause ringing in the ears, disorienting the victim.

He was aware of Andy next to him. Both Gavin and Andy tucked close to the stone wall. Several of the deputies regained their vision and began shooting back at them. Gavin returned fire. He struck a man in the shoulder, causing his gun to fly out of his hand. The deputy closest to him got off several rounds and then turned and ran down the passage. Immediately, the agents, along with Andy and Gavin, charged after them.

But several of the deputies continued firing, forcing the agents to retreat for the moment. Gavin spotted Miller holding his arm. He'd been shot and was bleeding. Shadow was nowhere in sight. Was he already halfway down the passage?

Gavin didn't know the layout of the mine. Neither did the agents.

"Andy, do you have any idea where this passage leads?" Gavin asked.

"Nowhere. The mine ends in about another couple of hundred feet. They're trapped and dangerous."

"And they have nothing to lose," Gavin said. "We need to try to negotiate."

They'd gone a couple of hundred feet into the tunnel. The deputies fired once more. Gavin and the rest of the team ducked behind the bend in the shaft.

"There's no way out for you. Give yourself up or die down here. The choice is yours," Wilson said.

More shots rang out. It didn't appear as if the men were giving up willingly.

"They'll run out of ammo soon enough," Gavin told the team.

"So we wait them out?" Wilson asked. "That could take a while."

"Let me try something." Gavin figured he had nothing to lose. He was going to try to reach out to Miller.

"Dan Miller, I know you're hurt. There's no way out of here alive. From the looks of that wound, I'd say you're losing a lot of blood. Are you ready to die for Shadow? Give him up to us, and maybe we can help you and your men with your sentences."

Silence followed, and Gavin believed he'd failed.

"He's not here to give up. He never was," Miller called out.

This piece of news scared the daylights out of Gavin. Had they been focused on the mine all this time only to allow Shadow to slip through the cracks?

"Where is he?" Gavin demanded.

"If I knew that, I'd be going after him myself. He told us to meet him here, only he never showed."

Gavin turned to Wilson. "I don't like it. Shadow is dangerous. We need to find him before he hurts someone else."

Wilson nodded. "Give yourself up, Miller. Tell your men to come out with their hands in the air."

It took only a matter of minutes before five deputies came forward with their hands held high, Miller included.

They were immediately handcuffed and taken away.

"We're going to need your offices for the interviews, sheriff," Wilson said.

Andy willingly agreed. "Whatever you need."

When Wilson got outside, his cell phone rang. Gavin could tell right away that the news was bad.

"Shadow was at the hospital. He killed the power. When two of my men went to investigate, he attacked the two agents standing guard outside of Paxton Hendricks's room. He was dressed as a doctor. That's why he was able to get close enough to inject both men with something to knock them out."

"Where's Jamie?" Gavin asked with fear in his heart.

"She's gone. Paxton's been shot. He's in critical condition. He's in surgery right now. They don't know if he's going to make it. My men are looking through video footage now to see if they can find where he took her."

Gavin turned and ran.

"Hold up, Gavin. I'm going with you," Andy told him and followed Gavin.

"Where are you going?" Wilson yelled after him.

"To find Jamie and get her away from Shadow."

"You don't know where she is. Dalton, wait up. We'll find her."

But Gavin didn't listen. He knew that if Shadow was desperate enough to shoot Paxton and take Jamie hostage, he had nothing to lose. He'd have a way out of there somehow, and there was only one place Gavin could think to look.

TWENTY

The second they exited the hospital, Shadow grabbed a handful of her hair and dragged her by it.

Jamie screamed and fought and kicked to free herself. If she got into the car with him, she believed she would soon be dead.

"Shut up!" Shadow yelled and grabbed her around the waist, clamping a hand over her mouth.

Jamie continued to kick and try to free herself, but Shadow hauled her over to a car waiting in the doctors' parking garage.

Shadow shoved her in the driver's side and got in after her. Jamie scrambled to the opposite door and grabbed the handle. Shadow snatched a handful of hair and forced her back next to him. "I don't think so. You and I have business to finish, so sit back and enjoy your last minutes here on earth."

With those words searing her heart, he put the

car in gear and roared out of the parking garage while Jamie tried to control the panic growing inside of her. She had to keep a clear head if she was going to survive.

"You can't get away. Every law enforcement agency in the state is looking for you. They'll have the roads blocked. You should give yourself up while you still have the chance."

Shadow spared her an angry glare. "You think so? I'm not going to give myself up. I'd be dead before I even got to trial. You think Jacob Ericson is going to let me live when he realizes I was the one who tried to kill him?" Shadow shook his head. "No, I'm not giving myself up."

"You'll never get away. You can't hide out in the county forever."

Jamie watched as Shadow turned onto the road leading up to Darlan Mountain. Where was he going?

He caught her watching him. "I have a helicopter waiting for me at the Dalton place. Once you help me find the evidence your crazy old uncle left Ava Dalton, then I'm out of here. I know the two of them were tight. She's the only one he'd trust with it. You're going to be my insurance once I find it."

She'd be dead once Shadow was safely out of the FBI's reach. She had to find a way to stall.

When they pulled into the Dalton drive, Jamie saw a helicopter waiting behind the house.

Shadow parked the car and forced her out beside him.

"Now, where would the old lady hide the evidence?"

Jamie stared at him in shock. "I have no idea what you're talking about."

Shadow's answer was to grab her arm and drag her along beside him to the chopper. The pilot hopped out when he saw them approaching.

"Did you have any problems getting up here undetected?"

The man shook his head. "Not really, but there's an awful lot of activity at the old Smithville Mine."

Shadow smiled to himself. "Good. Then they bought my diversion. By the time they take in Miller and the rest of his buffoons, we'll be long gone."

The pilot wasn't nearly as convinced. "We'd better be on our way soon. Once they figure out you're gone, they'll be watching every possible exit, and that includes the air. And there's more." He stopped long enough to look at Jamie, as if uncertain how much to say in front of her.

"Don't mind her. She'll be dead soon enough."

The reality of what Shadow had planned for her threatened to buckle her knees.

The pilot didn't seem to approve of the plan, but he knew who paid his salary. "*He's* looking for you. He knows the truth."

"How did he find out so soon?" Shadow asked, and all the color drained from his face.

"My guess is one of the buyers waiting for the supply talked. All the more reason we need to get out of here as soon as possible."

Shadow scowled at Jamie. "You heard him. Where is the evidence hidden?"

"Alright, I'll take you to it," she said and hoped she'd pulled off the lie. Shadow's eyes narrowed as if trying to decide if she was telling the truth.

The man was desperate, though, and willing to give her the chance to prove him wrong.

"Then do it. We don't have much time." Shadow still held her arm in a vice grip.

"It's in the house." Jamie had no idea where Ava might have put the thumb drive Paxton had given her, but she needed to buy herself some time and pray that Gavin and the FBI would figure out where she was. Before Shadow realized she was taking him on a wild goose chase and he ended her life right then and there.

Gavin got into Andy's patrol car and drove up the mountain with the FBI close behind.

After spotting the chopper heading up the

mountain, Gavin was convinced Shadow was going after the thumb drive containing Paxton's evidence. If they didn't reach the chopper before he found the drive and took off again, Jamie's life would be worthless to Shadow.

Andy stopped a short distance from the homestead. He didn't want to alert Shadow to their presence.

The rest of the vehicles halted behind them.

"We'll have to go the rest of the way on foot," Gavin said.

Sam nodded. "Lead on."

Gavin took point as they eased toward Ava's place.

Once they were on the edge of the property, Gavin took a second to survey his surroundings. He didn't see any movement.

"They could be inside. The chopper is still behind the house," Gavin said.

Sam indicated that four of the men should go check out the helicopter. "If the pilot's there, get him subdued and make sure that chopper isn't going anywhere. When you have him, alert me."

The men headed around back, and Sam directed a question to Gavin. "Does Jamie know where the evidence is hidden?"

"No, but if I know Jamie, she's trying to stall Shadow as long as she can."

"You think they're inside the house?" Sam asked.

"Probably."

Sam's phone vibrated and he answered it. "Good. We're storming the house." He ended the call. "They have the pilot. Let's get Shadow."

"You should know my grandmother installed monitors all around the property before she died. If they're still on, Shadow will know we're coming."

Sam nodded. "Then we'll have to be quick."

Gavin and the rest of the team eased up on the property. All the while, he prayed that Jamie was still safe.

Agents surrounded the house. When Sam gave the signal, they broke down the door and charged inside.

Gavin noticed right away that the monitors were off. He believed that was Jamie's handiwork.

They searched the house and came up empty. Gavin was scared to death he would be too late to find Jamie alive.

"The place is clear," Sam's men confirmed.

Sam turned to Gavin, frustrated. "Any idea where they might be?"

Gavin was about to say no until he remembered the old root cellar on his family's property.

"I know where they are." He told Sam about the cellar.

"Let's get going. This guy will know his only means of escape is gone. He's desperate."

Gavin's heart pounded in his chest as they slowly made their way to the cellar. Once they reached it, he could see fresh footprints.

He turned to Sam and whispered, "They're in there."

"Brock Shadow, this is the FBI," Sam announced. "We have the place surrounded. Let Jamie go and give yourself up."

"Jamie are you okay?" Gavin called out because he had to know.

"I'm okay," she confirmed. "It's dark in here but we have the chair."

Her words were cut off, but not before she'd given him a clue. They were near the single chair in the place.

Gavin told Sam what Jamie was trying to convey. "It's at the very back of the cellar."

"He's not going down without a fight. I think he'll try to kill her and himself." Sam didn't mince words, and each one sent terror through Gavin.

"We need to break down the door. Watch the

floor—it's uneven and the steps are dangerous," Gavin said.

Sam knew what he was doing. He counted to five, then they breached the place. Gavin was the first man through the door. A scuffle occurred, and then Shadow fired at him. Gavin ducked as the shots barely missed him. He didn't hesitate before firing two shots into Shadow's chest. The man fell to the ground.

As the rest of the agents poured in behind him, Gavin's only thought was for Jamie.

"We need some light in here!" Gavin yelled. Immediately flashlights lit up the place. Jamie was on the floor. She wasn't moving.

Gavin hurried to her side. "Jamie!" His voice broke with fear.

And then she moved. "I'm okay," she managed and slowly sat up.

Gavin drew her close. "Are you hurt?"

She shook her head against his chest. "No, I'm not hurt. I was just so scared." She shivered against him. He lifted her in his arms and carried her out of the cellar.

"Can you stand on your own?" he asked.

She smiled up at him. "I can."

He slowly set her down beside him. "I was so afraid I'd lost you." His voice shook as he framed her face and took in everything about her lovely face.

She hugged him close. "I'm okay. He shot Uncle Paxton, though." She started to cry. He couldn't imagine how worried she was.

Gavin held her and whispered, "I know. He's in surgery."

They watched as Shadow's body was brought out of the cellar.

"He was going to kill me. He told his pilot that once he found the evidence, he was flying out of the area and he was going to kill me."

Gavin brushed back the hair from her face. "He's not going to hurt you ever again." He was so grateful that God had brought her safely through.

Sam stopped next to them. "Sorry you had to go through that, Ms. Hendricks."

She nodded. "Is there any news on my uncle?"

"There is. I just heard. He's out of surgery and holding his own. I'll have one of my men take you there."

"I can do it." Andy stepped forward.

Sam agreed. "Good. We'll be here for a while processing the scene."

They turned to go, but Jamie stopped suddenly. "I almost forgot, with everything that happened. My uncle told me that he hid the rest of the heroin behind our place. It's buried under the plowed area around back."

Gavin couldn't believe it. Paxton had been expecting something bad to happen and was prepared for it. The old guy never ceased to surprise him.

Sam nodded. "I'll have my men get to it right away."

As they left the place, Gavin marveled at all that had happened over the past few days. He took Jamie's hand in his, still amazed that they were both alive. He had her back, and he wasn't about to let anything get in their way ever again.

Once they reached the hospital, Andy went with them up to where Paxton was recovering.

Gavin and Jamie went inside, and Andy stood by the door.

Jamie saw how bad her uncle looked, and hurried to Paxton's side. She took his hand in hers, tears falling down her face.

They'd been there only a short time when the doctor came to visit them.

"Is he going to be okay?" Jamie asked, getting to her feet, anticipating the worst.

The doctor smiled kindly. "I believe he will. He's a strong man who came through the surgery well. The next few hours will be the deciding factor, but I believe he will be just fine."

Gavin touched her arm, and Jamie curled into him.

"It's going to be okay," he murmured. "Paxton's too stubborn to die."

She laughed and nodded against his chest.

Andy cleared his throat, and Gavin looked over at him.

"I think I'll head back to the station. I'll check in with you in a little while."

Gavin waved and waited until Andy was gone before he cupped Jamie's chin and tipped her head back before kissing her with all his heart.

"I love you, Jamie Hendricks, and I want to spend the rest of my life with you in Louisville. What I do for a living doesn't matter. I just want to do it with you."

Surprised, she smiled up at him. "I love you, Gavin Dalton, but I'm ready to come home again and start our lives together in the only place that will ever be home for either of us. Let's come back home to Darlan."

EPILOGUE

One year later...

Jamie smiled up at the man who'd always had her heart, as he was sworn in as a sheriff's deputy for Darlan County. Nothing her wildest imagination could have created had prepared her for this future.

When Andy first proposed the idea of Gavin becoming his deputy and working alongside him to clean up Darlan County for good, Gavin hadn't jumped at the opportunity until he and Jamie talked it over.

She and Gavin had gotten married a few months after Paxton was released from the hospital. She was so happy to be his wife. Leaving the law firm in Louisville hadn't been as difficult as she'd feared. She'd made sure her caseload was cleared and then come back home to open her own practice in Darlan, looking out for those wrongly accused.

Gavin had known being a deputy was a tremendous opportunity for him to make something good come from what had happened to both their fathers. Charles would have been so proud. So would Noah.

With his home destroyed, Paxton was determined to rebuild. He'd bought himself a camper trailer, and with Gavin's help, he was building a new house on the property.

Jamie and Gavin had settled into Ava's old house, and Jamie couldn't have been happier. In fact, she had a special piece of news to share with her husband and knew just the right place to tell him.

They left the ceremony and drove home. Once Gavin parked the car, Jamie got out and took her husband's hand in hers.

"I'm so proud of you, babe. Do you feel like sitting outside for a bit?"

He smiled his answer, and they headed to Ava's favorite spot: the bench behind the house.

Once they were seated, Gavin put his arm around her and tugged her close. "When I left here all those years ago, I could never have imagined being this happy again."

"Me, either." She drew in a breath. "I have some news," she said in a tiny voice and prayed he would be as happy as she was. They'd talked about having children…one day.

Gavin turned to her. "What is it?"

It took all her strength to force the words out. "I'm pregnant. We're going to have a child together." She looked into his eyes waiting for his response, her heart in her throat.

"You're pregnant?" Unexpected tears filled his eyes, and he took her in his arms and kissed her with all his heart.

"Are you happy?" she asked in between kisses.

He looked at her in wonderment. "Happy? I'm more than happy. I'm blessed beyond measure. I can't imagine living my life anywhere but here with you." He touched her stomach. "And with the child God has chosen to bless us with."

She couldn't, either.

* * * * *

Dear Reader,

Have you ever faced a situation in your life from which there seemed to be no way out? It loomed in front of you like an insurmountable mass? I think most of us go through periods in our lives where we must challenge the mountains set before us.

Gavin Dalton and Jamie Hendricks have faced such mountains in their past. As teenagers, their romance was shattered to pieces when Jamie's father was accused of killing Gavin's. What stood between them was just too big to overcome, and so they parted.

Ten years later, Jamie and Gavin are reunited once more in the search to find Jamie's missing uncle, who has disappeared up on Darlan Mountain. With the past and its ugly secrets still standing firmly between them, it's a struggle for Jamie to trust Gavin. When she needed him to believe in her and her father, he didn't. Is it possible for her to put aside the hurt from the past and work with Gavin to bring Paxton home alive? And can the love they once had for each other find its place in their future?

Grave Peril is a story is about slaying the giants in our lives. Sometimes we think we know what lies ahead for us. We let the past and our failures defeat us, but God has a better plan. If we trust Him to help us slay those giants, He'll bring us through to a brighter future.

I so love hearing from readers. Email me at maryjalfordauthor@gmail.com or write me c/o Love Inspired, 195 Broadway, 24th Floor, New York, NY, 10007. Visit me at www.MaryAlford.net and at www.facebook.com/MaryAlfordAuthor.

Warmest blessings,
Mary

Get 4 FREE REWARDS!

We'll send you 2 FREE Books plus 2 FREE Mystery Gifts.

Love Inspired® books feature contemporary inspirational romances with Christian characters facing the challenges of life and love.

FREE Value Over **$20**

Get 4 FREE REWARDS!

We'll send you 2 FREE Books plus 2 FREE Mystery Gifts.

Harlequin® Heartwarming™ Larger-Print books feature traditional values of home, family, community and most of all—love.

FREE
Value Over
$20

YES! Please send me 2 FREE Harlequin® Heartwarming™ Larger-Print novels and my 2 FREE mystery gifts (gifts worth about $10 retail). After receiving them, if I don't wish to receive any more books, I can return the shipping statement marked "cancel." If I don't cancel, I will receive 4 brand-new larger-print novels every month and be billed just $5.49 per book in the U.S. or $6.24 per book in Canada. That's a savings of at least 19% off the cover price. It's quite a bargain! Shipping and handling is just 50¢ per book in the U.S. and 75¢ per book in Canada*. I understand that accepting the 2 free books and gifts places me under no obligation to buy anything. I can always return a shipment and cancel at any time. The free books and gifts are mine to keep no matter what I decide.

161/361 IDN GMY3

Name (please print)

Address   Apt. #

City   State/Province   Zip/Postal Code

Mail to the **Reader Service:**
IN U.S.A.: P.O. Box 1341, Buffalo, NY 14240-8531
IN CANADA: P.O. Box 603, Fort Erie, Ontario L2A 5X3

Want to try two free books from another series? Call 1-800-873-8635 or visit www.ReaderService.com.

HOME *on the* RANCH

READERSERVICE.COM

Manage your account online!

- Review your order history
- Manage your payments
- Update your address

---

*We've designed the
Reader Service website
just for you.*

Enjoy all the features!

- Discover new series available to you, and read excerpts from any series.
- Respond to mailings and special monthly offers.
- Browse the Bonus Bucks catalog and online-only exculsives.
- Share your feedback.

Visit us at:

ReaderService.com

RS16R